D0118979

FAR OUT
FAIRY TALES

STONE ARCH BOOKS
a capstone imprint

PLAYER 1:

LITTLE GRUFF,
THE NINJA-GOAT

STATS:
LEVEL: 10
INTELLIGENCE: 2
STRENGTH: 1
AGILITY: 5
LUCK: 2

STRENGTHS:
Quick-hoofed and competitive

WEAKNESSES:
Shiny objects, paying attention

PLAYER 2:

MIDDLE GRUFF,
THE WIZARD-GOAT

STATS:
LEVEL: 11
INTELLIGENCE: 6
STRENGTH: 1
AGILITY: 2
LUCK: 2

STRENGTHS:
Smart and observant

WEAKNESSES:
Bossy

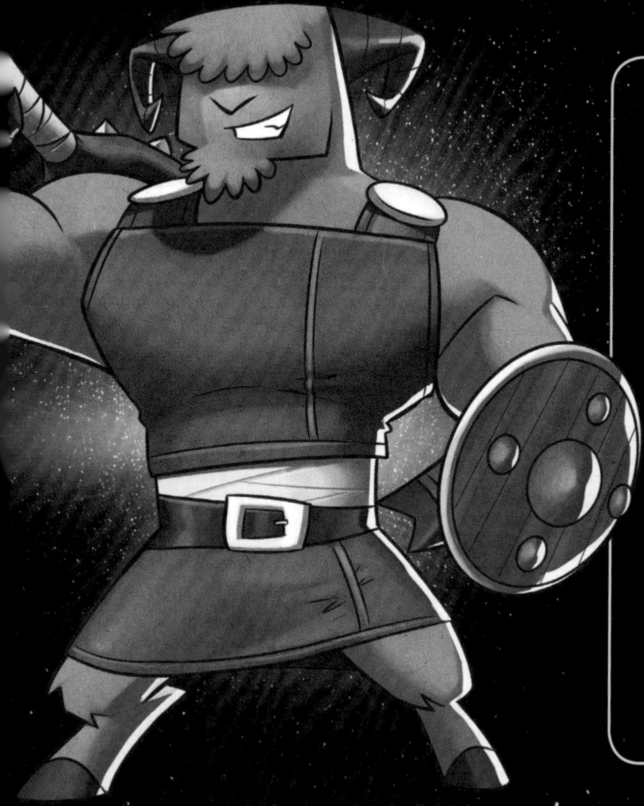

PLAYER 3:

BIG GRUFF,
THE WARRIOR-GOAT

STATS:
LEVEL: 12
INTELLIGENCE: 1
STRENGTH: 6
AGILITY: 3
LUCK: 2

STRENGTHS:
Determined

WEAKNESSES:
Stubborn

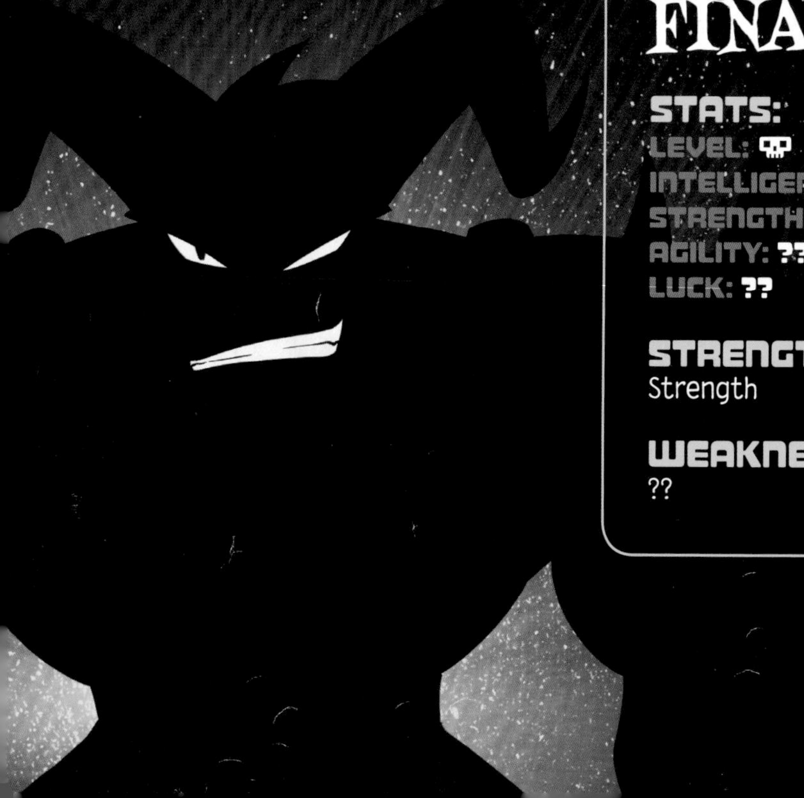

FINAL BOSS

STATS:
LEVEL: ☠
INTELLIGENCE: ??
STRENGTH: 99
AGILITY: ??
LUCK: ??

STRENGTHS:
Strength

WEAKNESSES:
??

in...

Far Out Fairy Tales is published by
Stone Arch Books
A Capstone Imprint
1710 Roe Crest Drive, North Mankato,
Minnesota 56003
www.capstonepub.com

Cataloging-in-Publication Data is
available at the Library of Congress
website.
Hardcover ISBN: 978-1-4342-9649-8
Paperback ISBN: 978-1-4342-9653-5

Summary: Three billy goats named
Gruff travel to the hillside to snack
on some grass — when they suddenly
find themselves trapped in a video
game! The three billy bros become a
Warrior, a Ninja, and a Wizard! But
the hillside is gone, and a dangerous
dungeon filled with creepy-crawlies
and fantastical foes has taken its
place! What adventures await?

Lettering by Jaymes Reed.

Designer: Bob Lentz
Editor: Sean Tulien
Managing Editor: Donald Lemke
Creative Director: Heather Kindseth
Editorial Director: Michael Dahl
Publisher: Ashley C. Andersen Zantop

Printed in Canada.
092014   008478FRS15

FAR OUT FAIRY TALES

SUPER
BILLY GOATS
GRUFF

A GRAPHIC NOVEL

BY SEAN TULIEN

ILLUSTRATED BY FERNANDO CANO

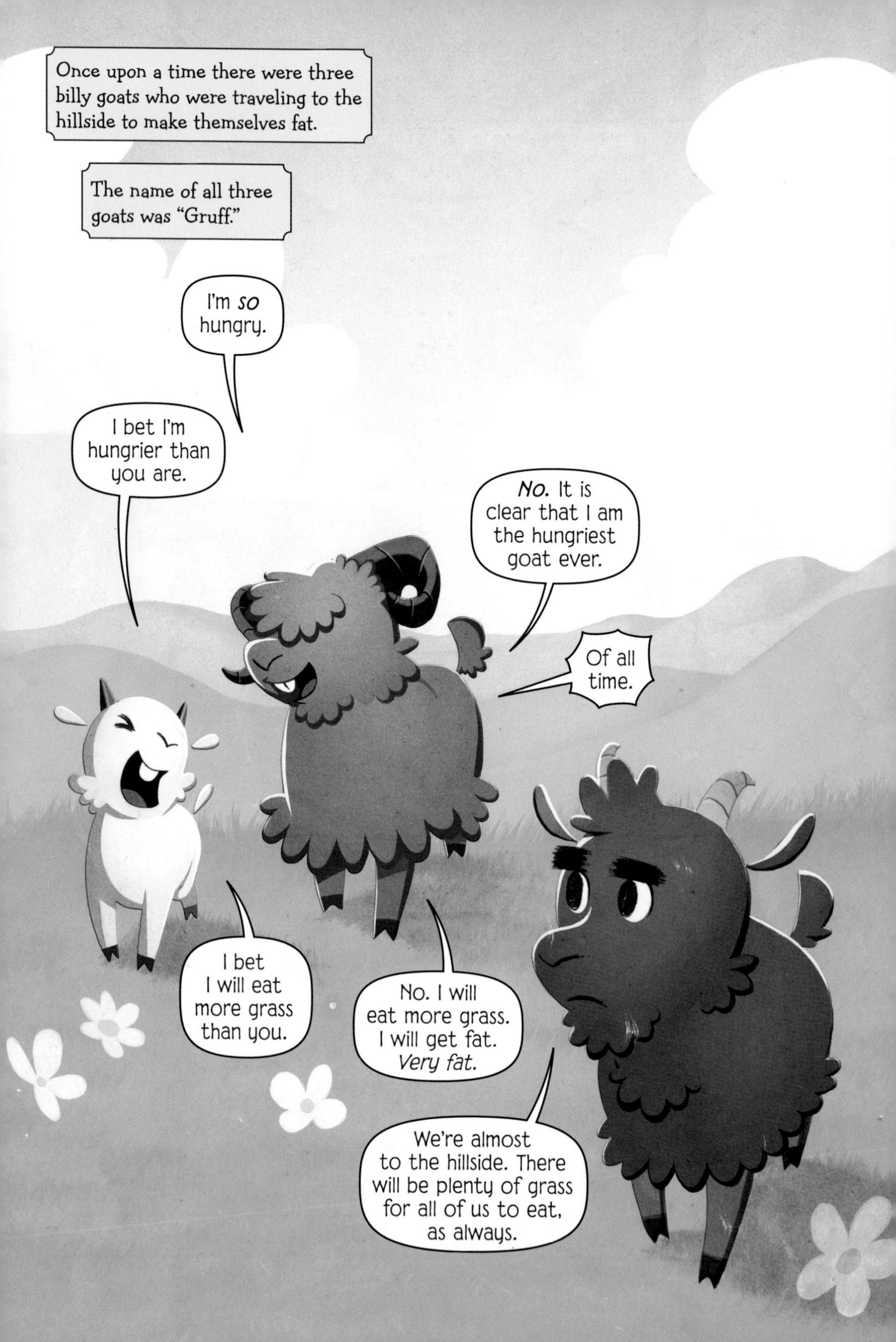
Once upon a time there were three billy goats who were traveling to the hillside to make themselves fat.
The name of all three goats was "Gruff."
I'm *so* hungry.
I bet I'm hungrier than you are.
No. It is clear that I am the hungriest goat ever.
Of all time.
I bet I will eat more grass than you.
No. I will eat more grass. I will get fat. *Very fat.*
We're almost to the hillside. There will be plenty of grass for all of us to eat, as always.

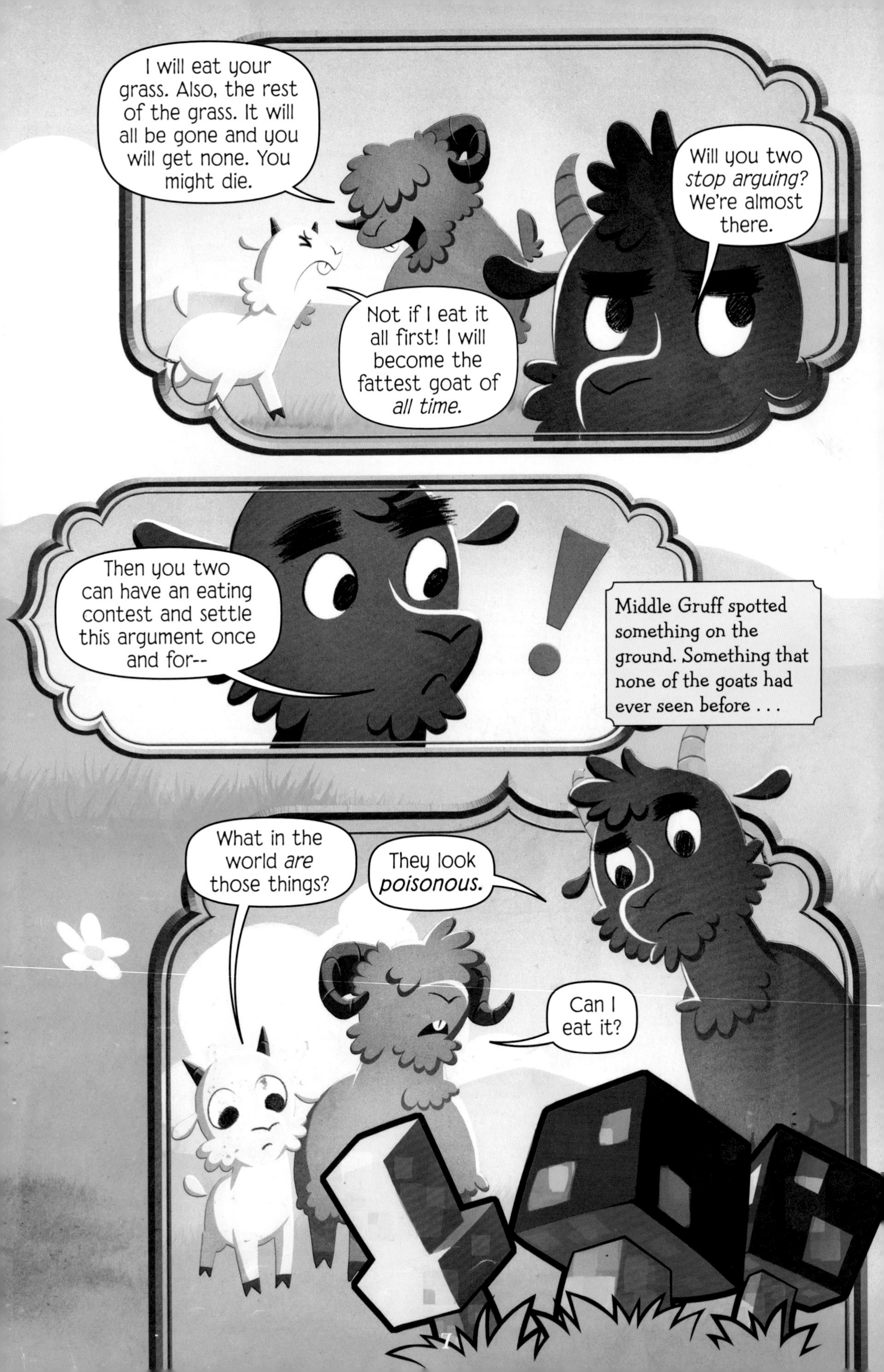
I will eat your grass. Also, the rest of the grass. It will all be gone and you will get none. You might die.
Will you two *stop arguing?* We're almost there.
Not if I eat it all first! I will become the fattest goat of *all time.*
Then you two can have an eating contest and settle this argument once and for--
!
Middle Gruff spotted something on the ground. Something that none of the goats had ever seen before . . .
What in the world *are* those things?
They look ***poisonous.***
Can I eat it?

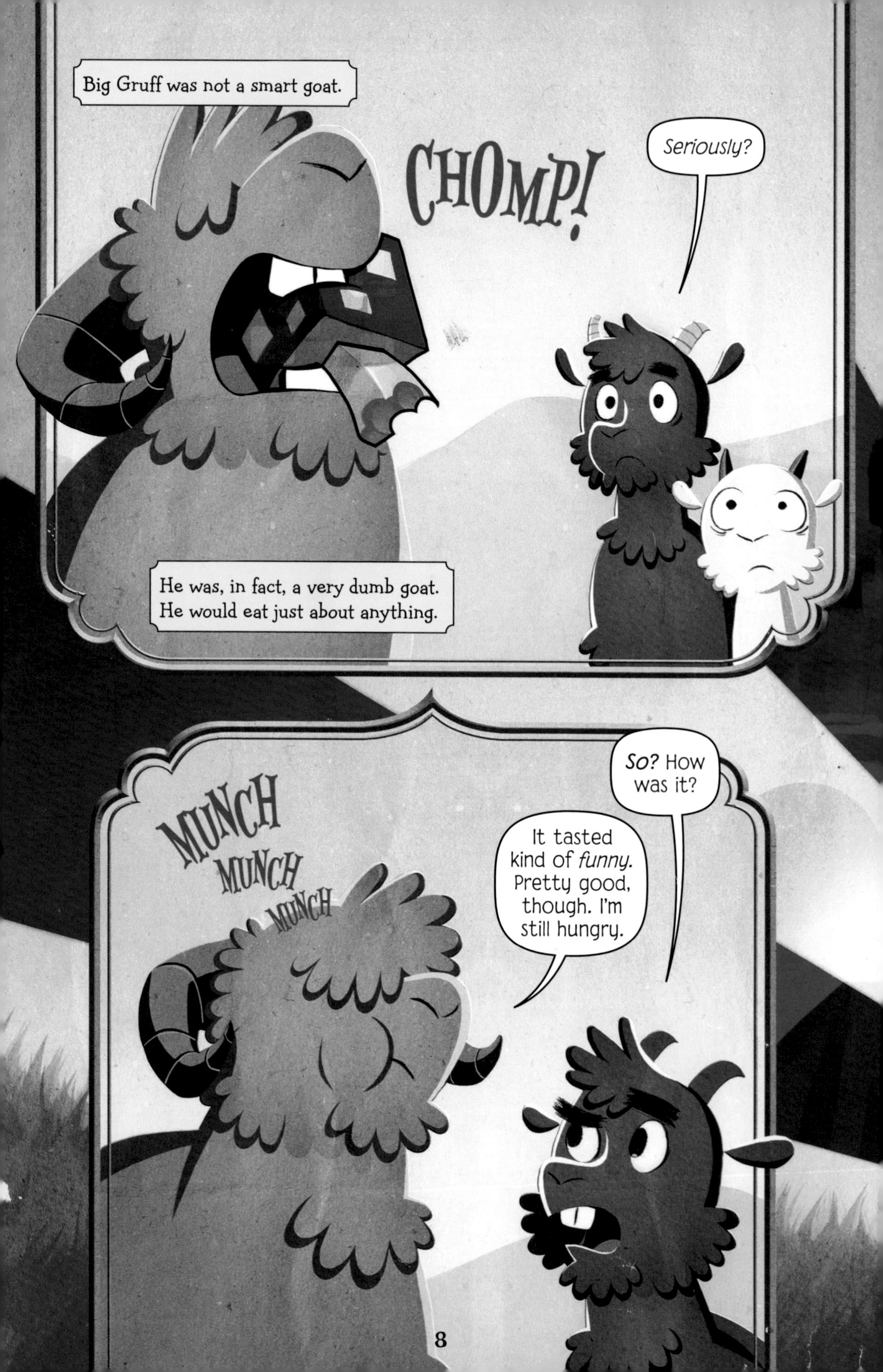
Big Gruff was not a smart goat.
CHOMP!
Seriously?
He was, in fact, a very dumb goat. He would eat just about anything.
MUNCH MUNCH MUNCH
So? How was it?
It tasted kind of *funny*. Pretty good, though. I'm still hungry.

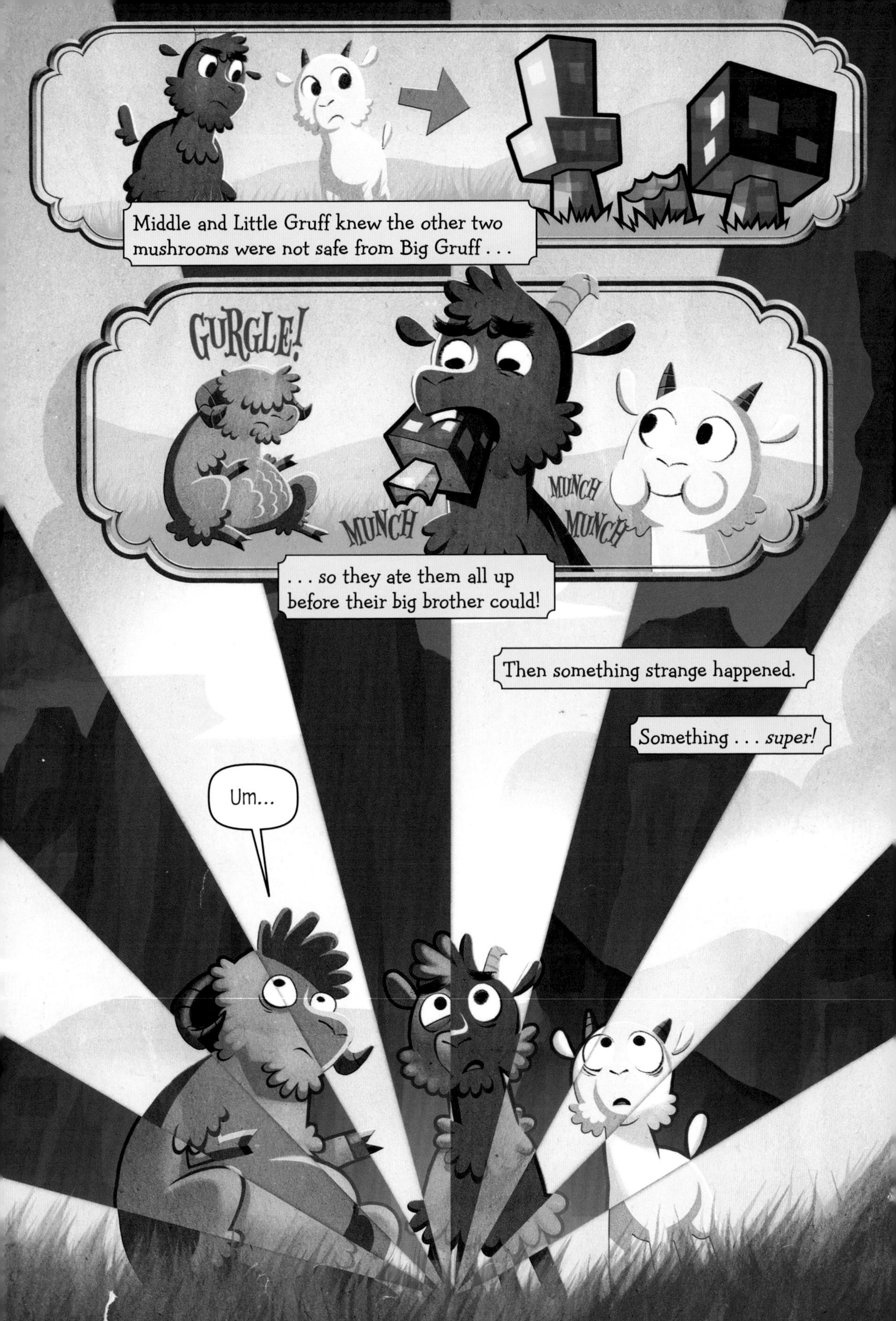

Middle and Little Gruff knew the other two mushrooms were not safe from Big Gruff . . .
GURGLE!
MUNCH
MUNCH
MUNCH
. . . so they ate them all up before their big brother could!
Then something strange happened.
Something . . . *super!*
Um...

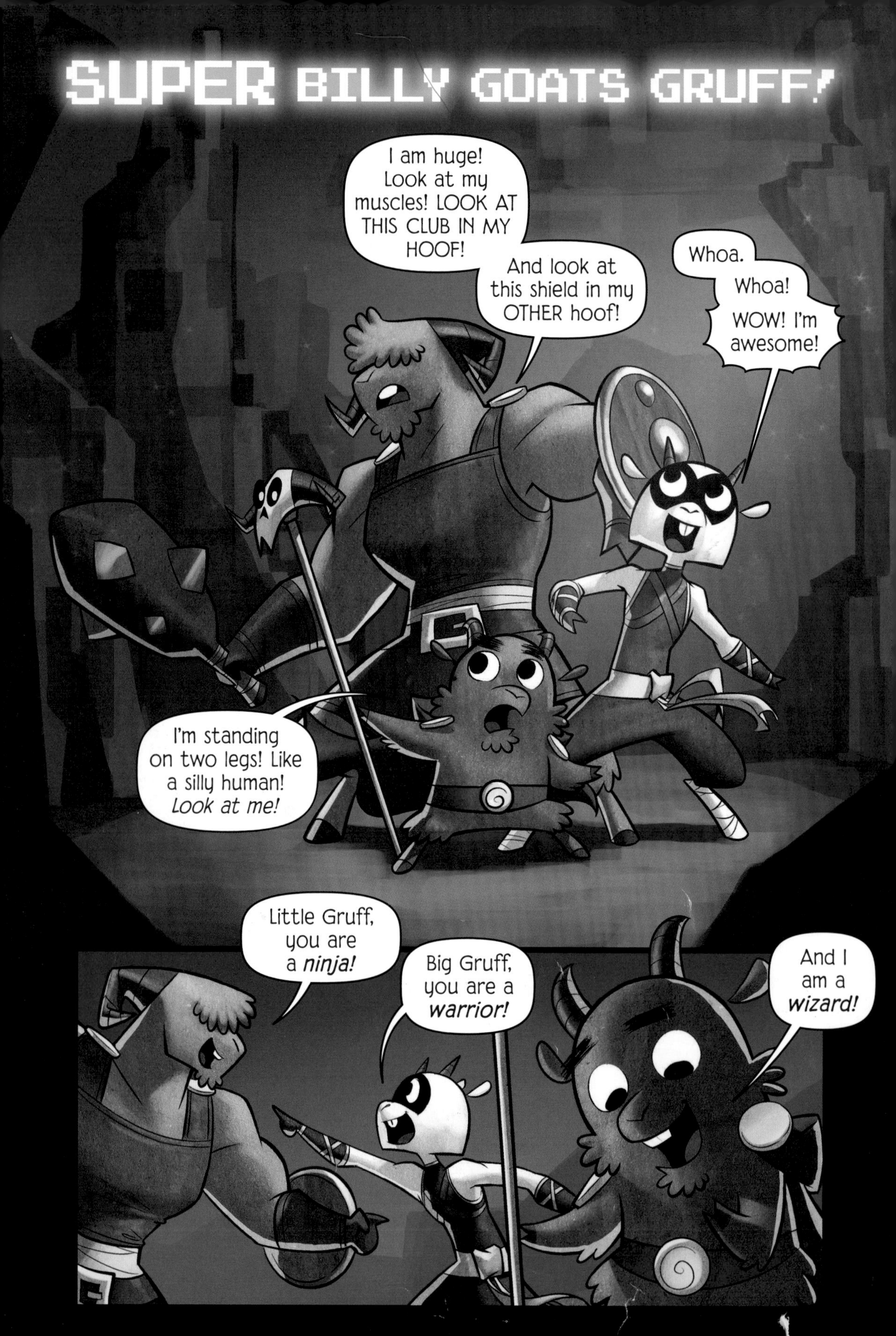
SUPER BILLY GOATS GRUFF!
I am huge! Look at my muscles! LOOK AT THIS CLUB IN MY HOOF!
And look at this shield in my OTHER hoof!
Whoa.
Whoa!
WOW! I'm awesome!
I'm standing on two legs! Like a silly human! *Look at me!*
Little Gruff, you are a *ninja!*
Big Gruff, you are a *warrior!*
And I am a *wizard!*

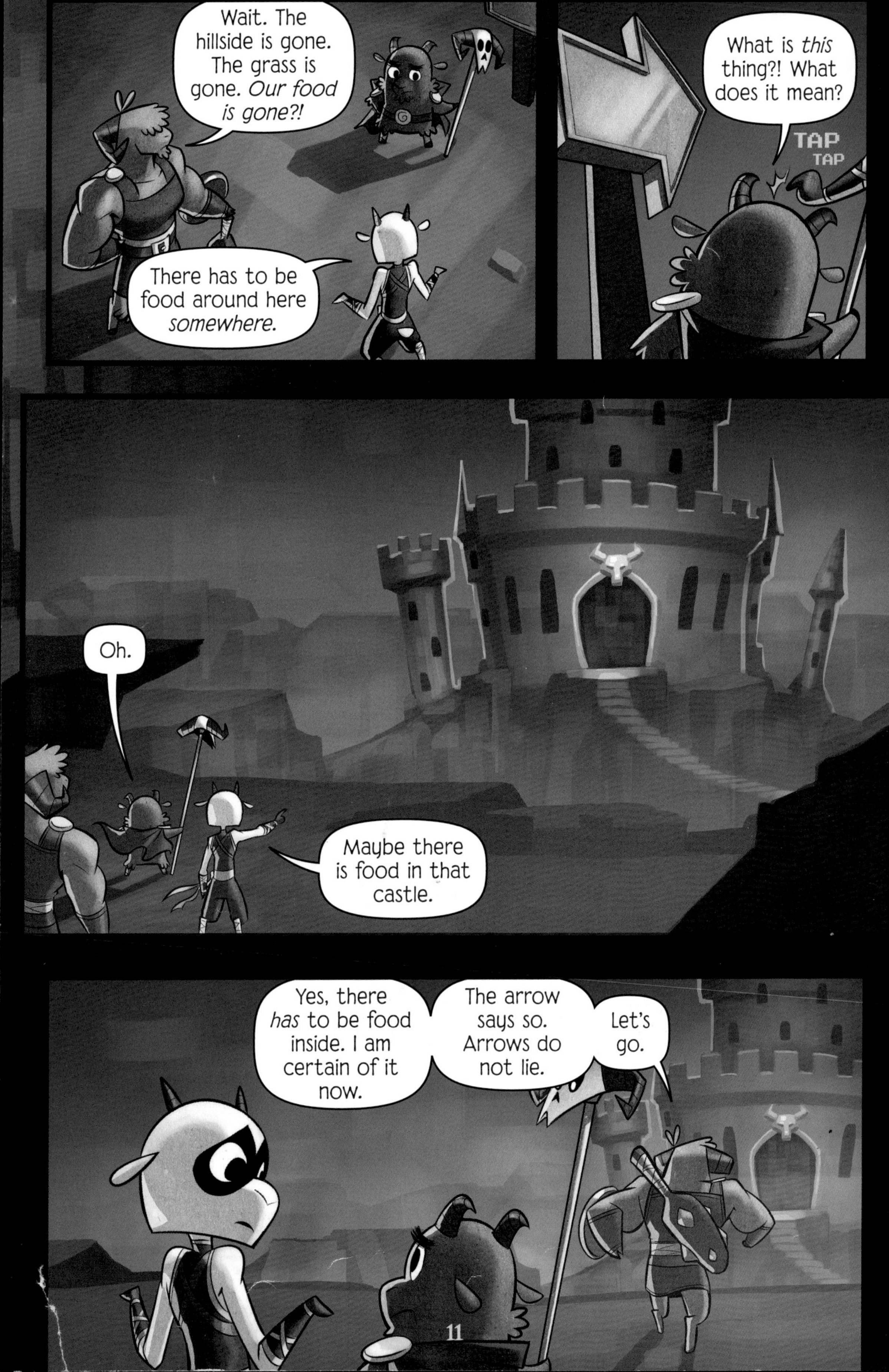
Wait. The hillside is gone. The grass is gone. *Our food is gone?!*
There has to be food around here *somewhere.*
What is *this* thing?! What does it mean?
TAP
TAP
Oh.
Maybe there is food in that castle.
Yes, there *has* to be food inside. I am certain of it now.
The arrow says so. Arrows do not lie.
Let's go.

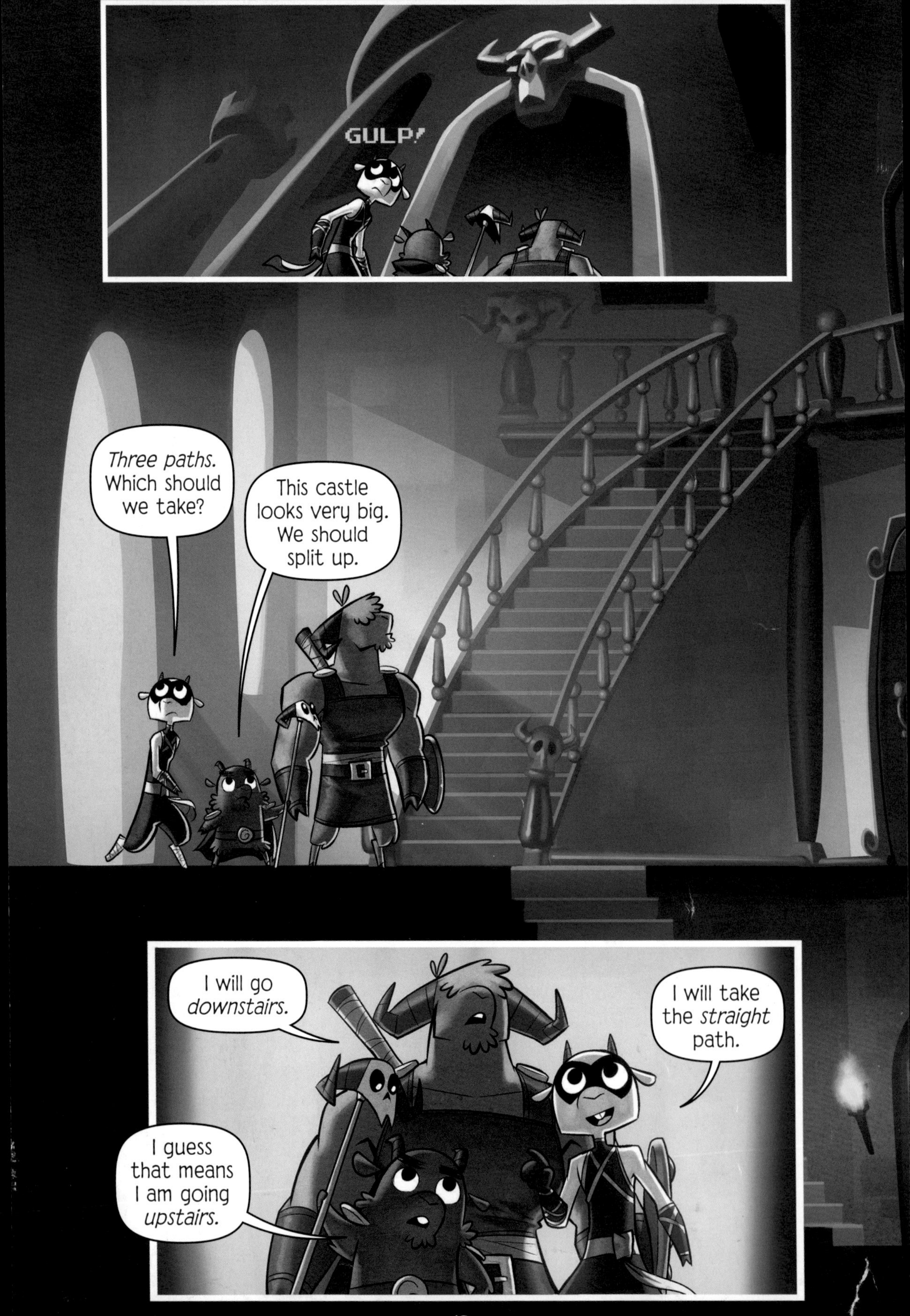
GULP!
Three paths. Which should we take?
This castle looks very big. We should split up.
I will go *downstairs.*
I will take the *straight* path.
I guess that means I am going *upstairs.*

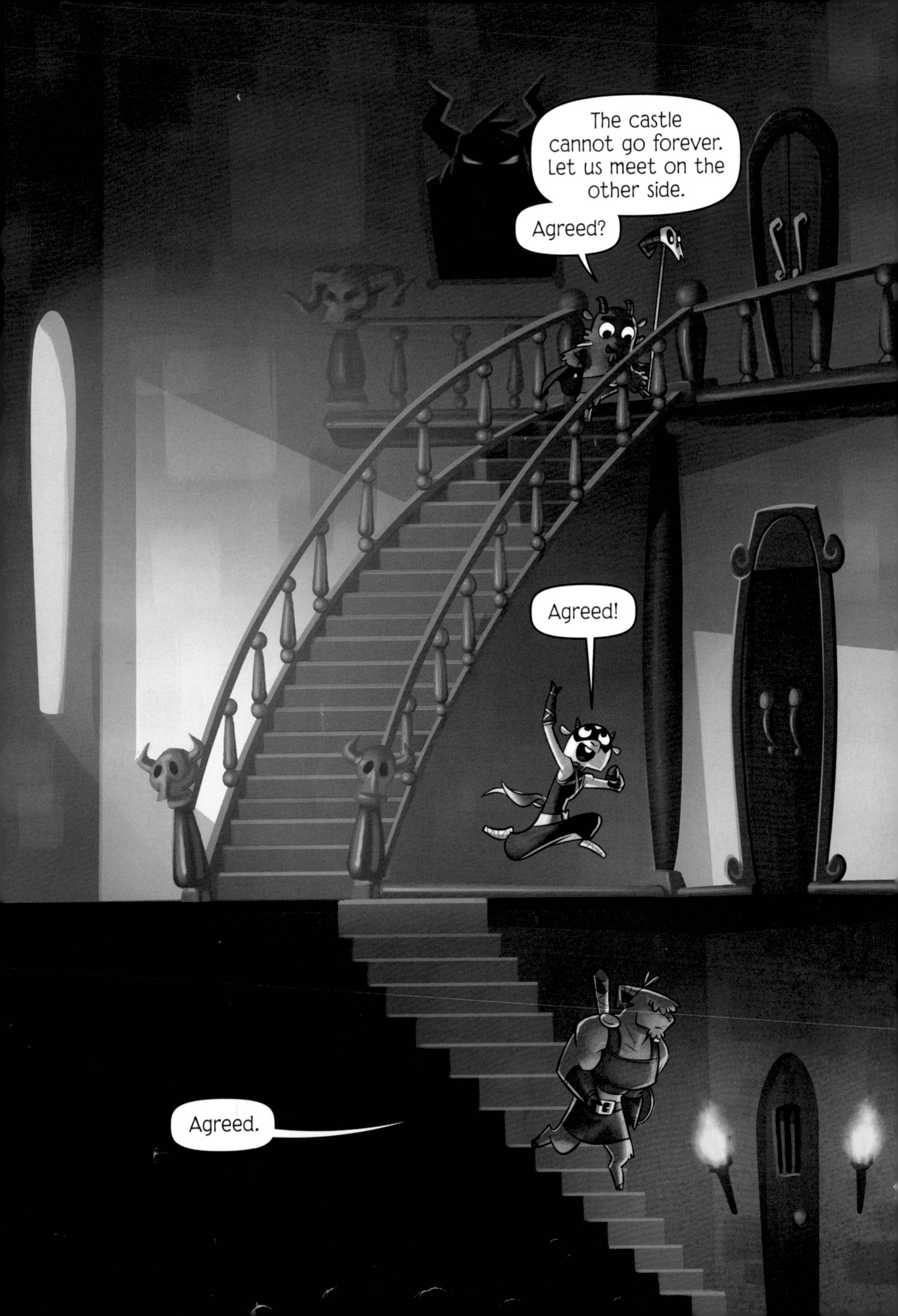
The castle cannot go forever. Let us meet on the other side.
Agreed?
Agreed!
Agreed.

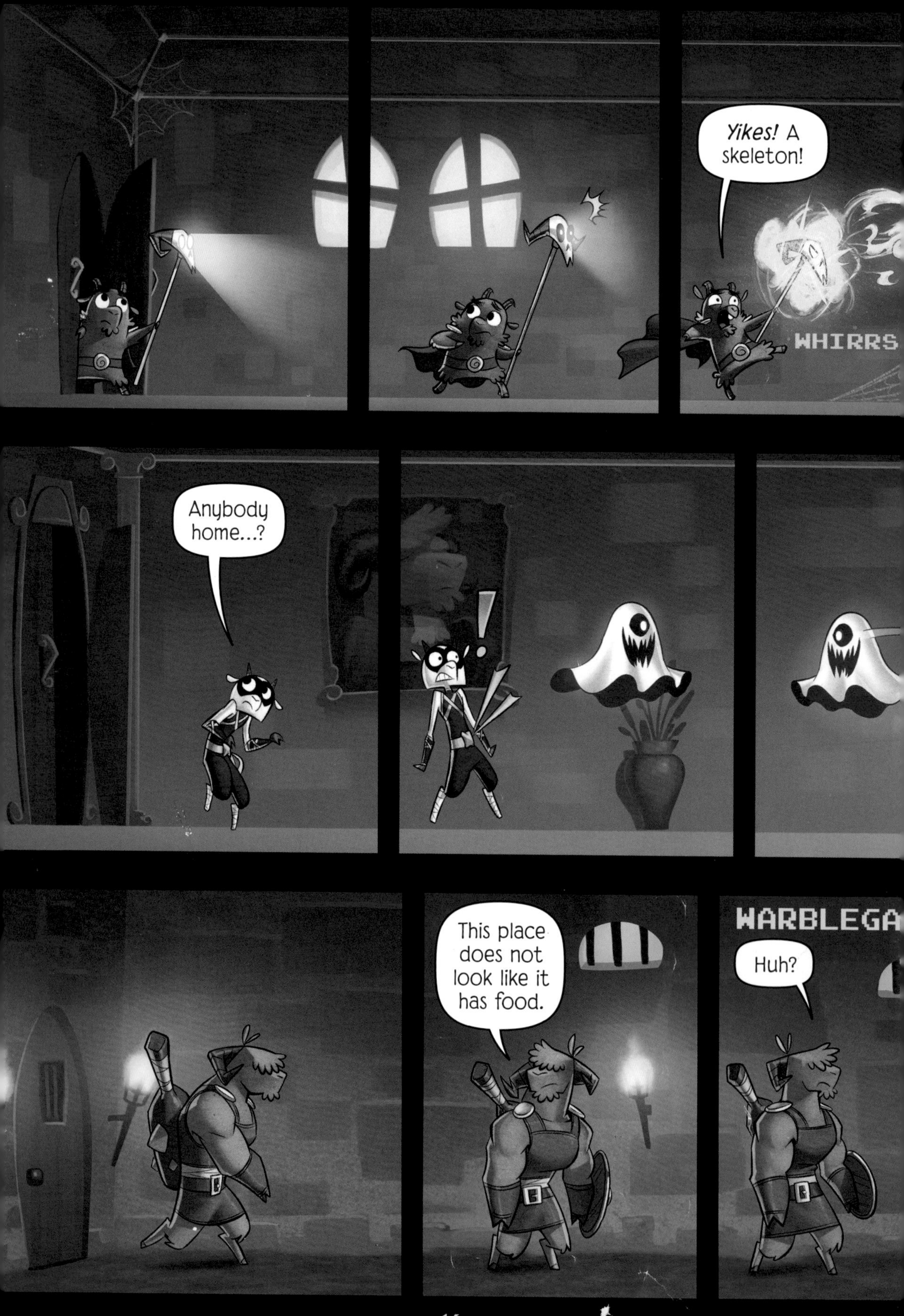

Yikes! A skeleton!
WHIRRS
Anybody home...?
This place does not look like it has food.
WARBLEGA
Huh?

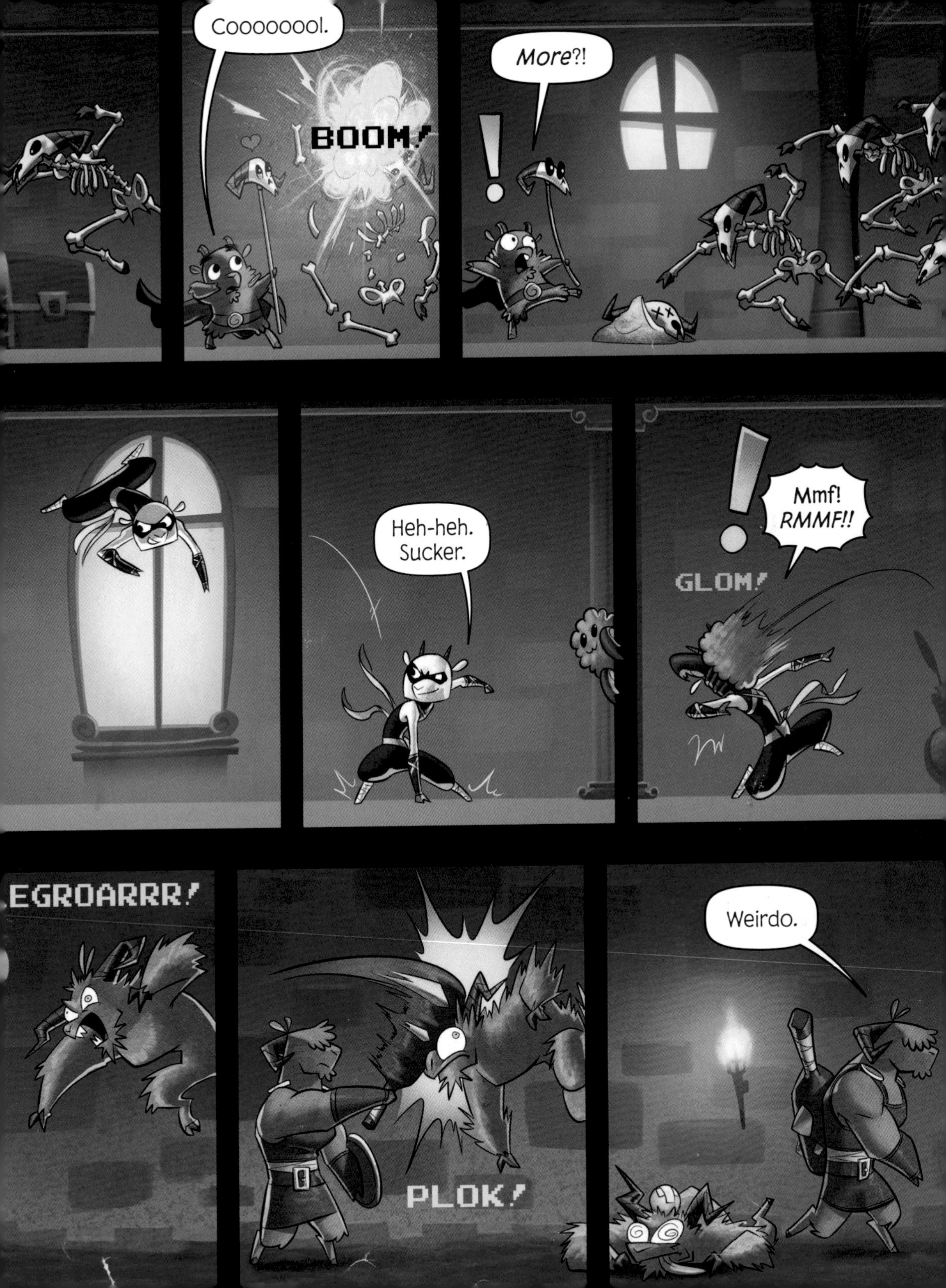
Coooooool.
BOOM!
More?!
Heh-heh.
Sucker.
GLOM!
Mmf!
RMMF!!
EGROARRR!
PLOK!
Weirdo.

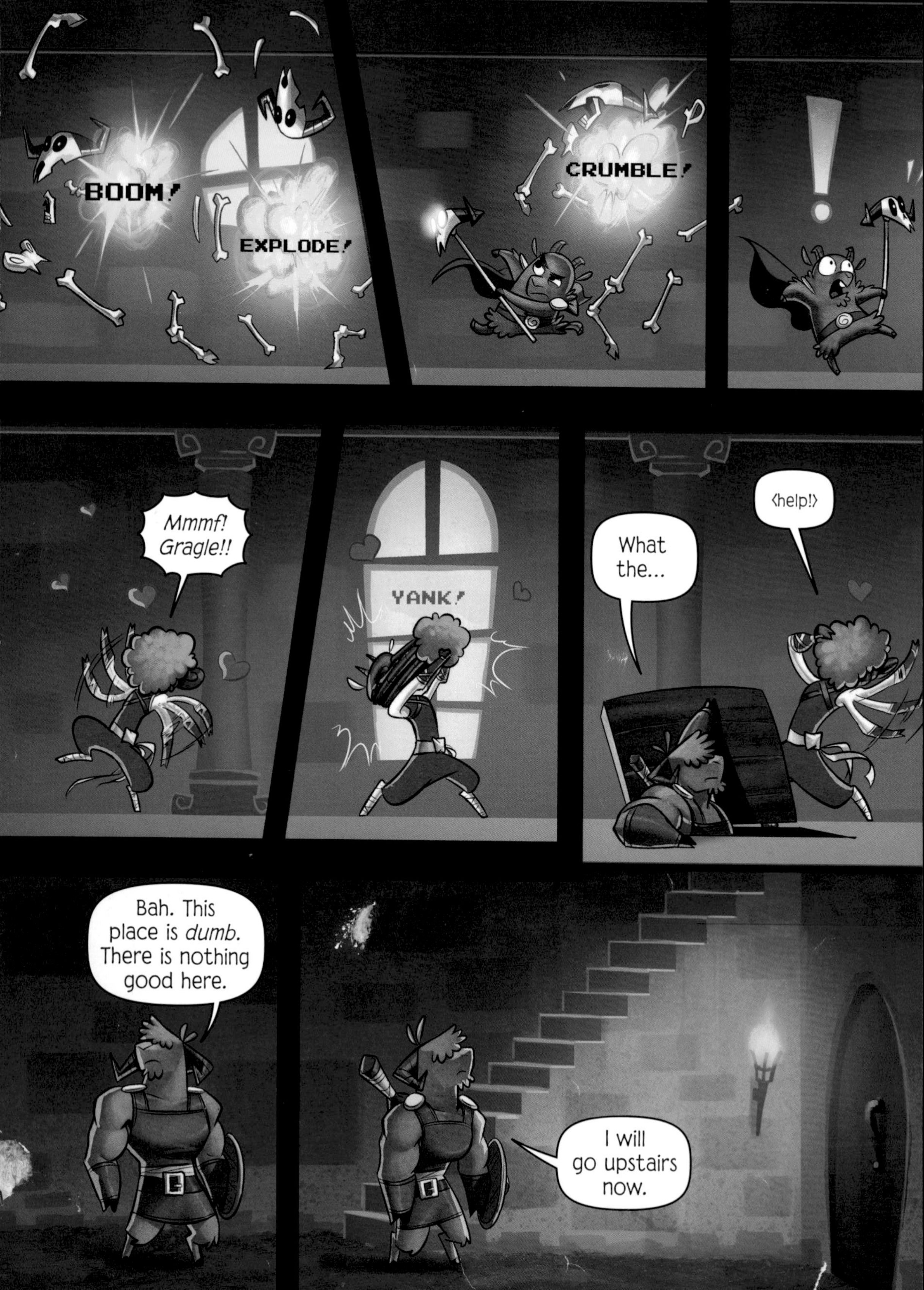
BOOM!
EXPLODE!
CRUMBLE!
!
Mmmf! Gragle!!
YANK!
What the...
<help!>
Bah. This place is *dumb*. There is nothing good here.
I will go upstairs now.

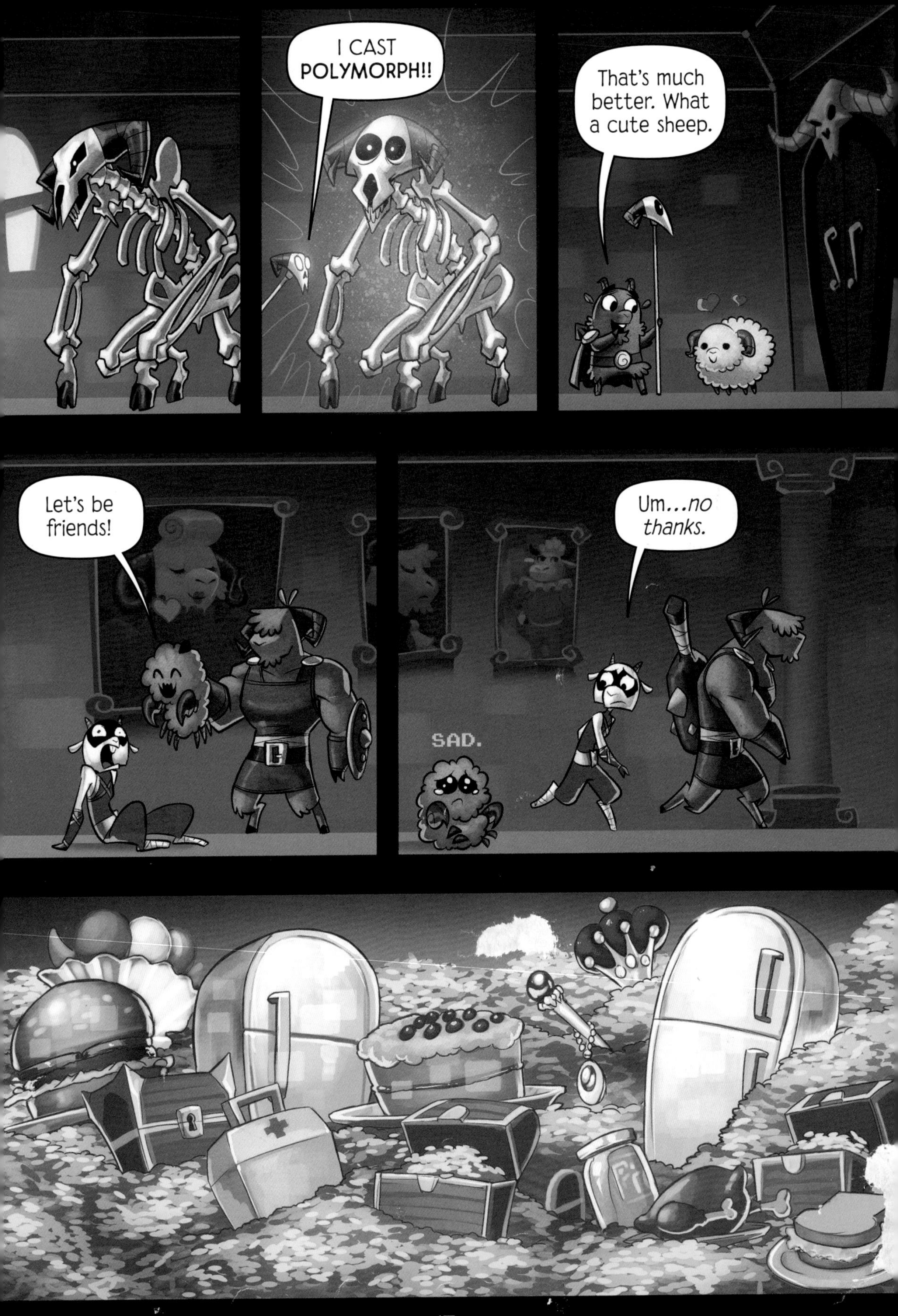
I CAST **POLYMORPH!!**
That's much better. What a cute sheep.
Let's be friends!
Um...*no thanks.*
SAD.

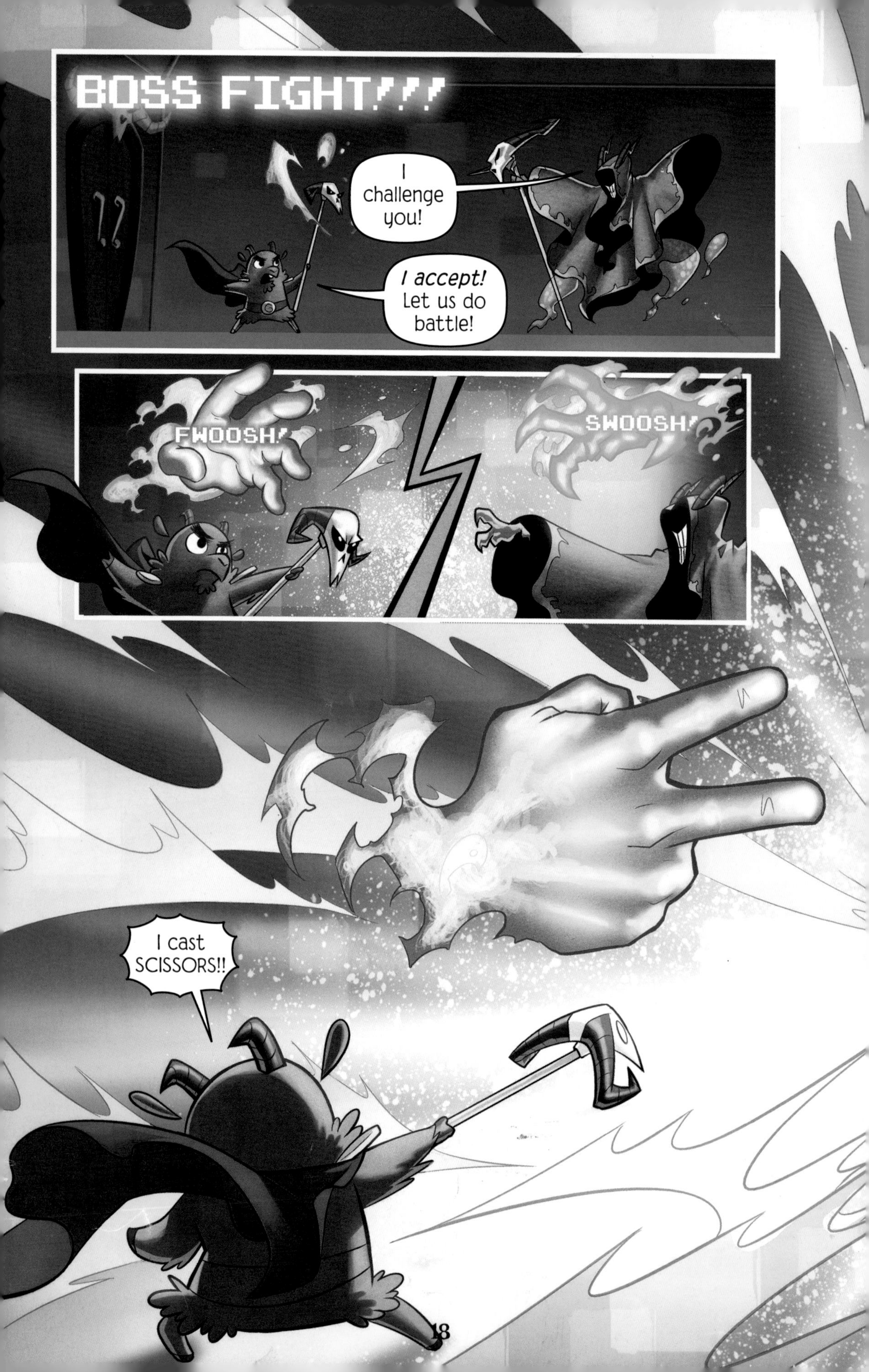
BOSS FIGHT!!!
I challenge you!
I accept! Let us do battle!
FWOOSH!
SWOOSH!
I cast SCISSORS!!

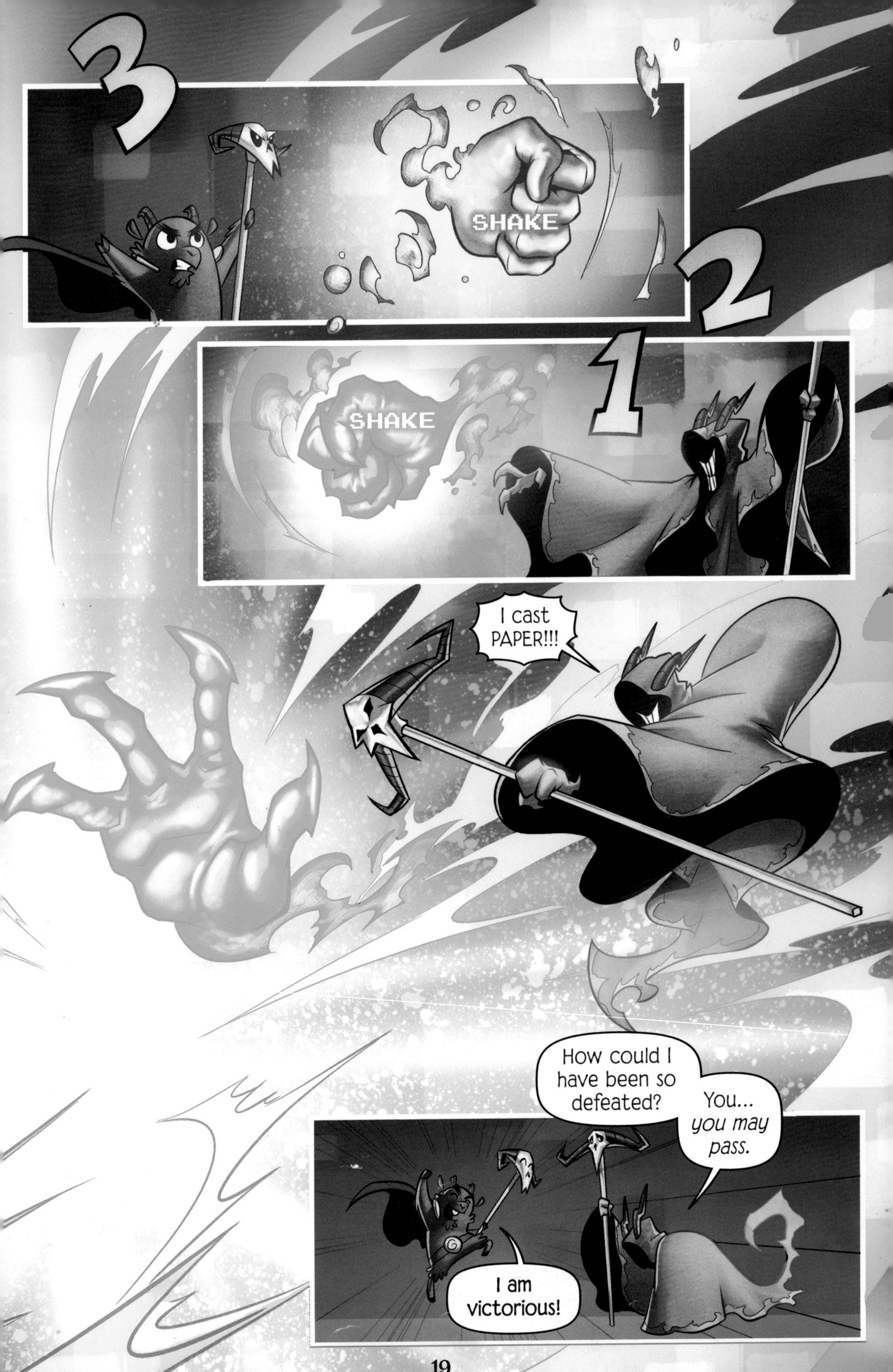
3
SHAKE
2
1
SHAKE
I cast PAPER!!!
How could I have been so defeated?
You... *you may pass.*
I am victorious!

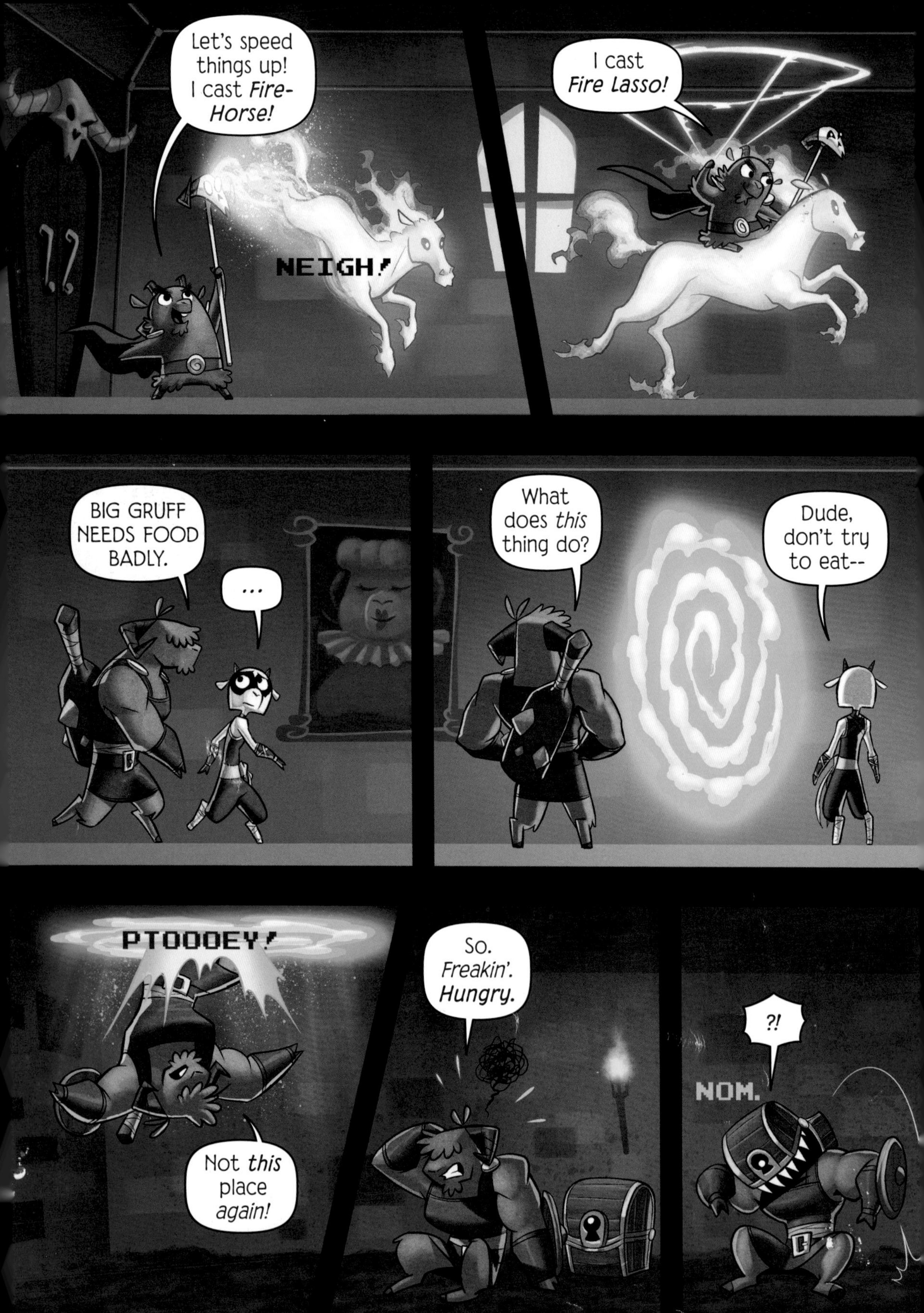
Let's speed things up! I cast *Fire-Horse!*
NEIGH!
I cast *Fire Lasso!*
BIG GRUFF NEEDS FOOD BADLY.
...
What does *this* thing do?
Dude, don't try to eat--
PTOOOEY!
Not *this* place *again!*
So. *Freakin'. Hungry.*
?!
NOM.

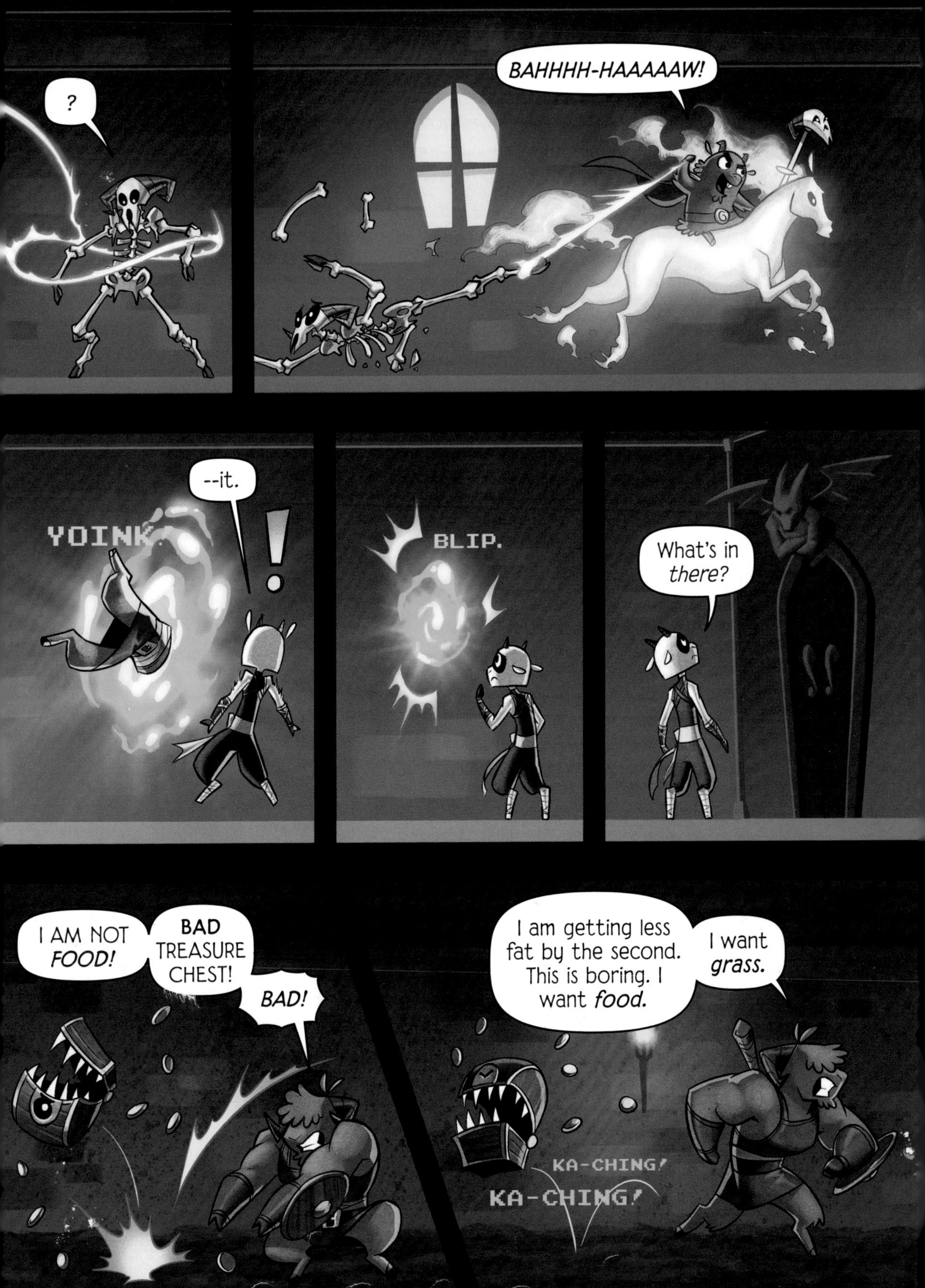
?
BAHHHH-HAAAAAW!
YOINK!
--it.
!
BLIP.
What's in *there?*
I AM NOT *FOOD!*
BAD TREASURE CHEST!
BAD!
I am getting less fat by the second. This is boring. I want *food.*
I want *grass.*
KA-CHING!
KA-CHING!

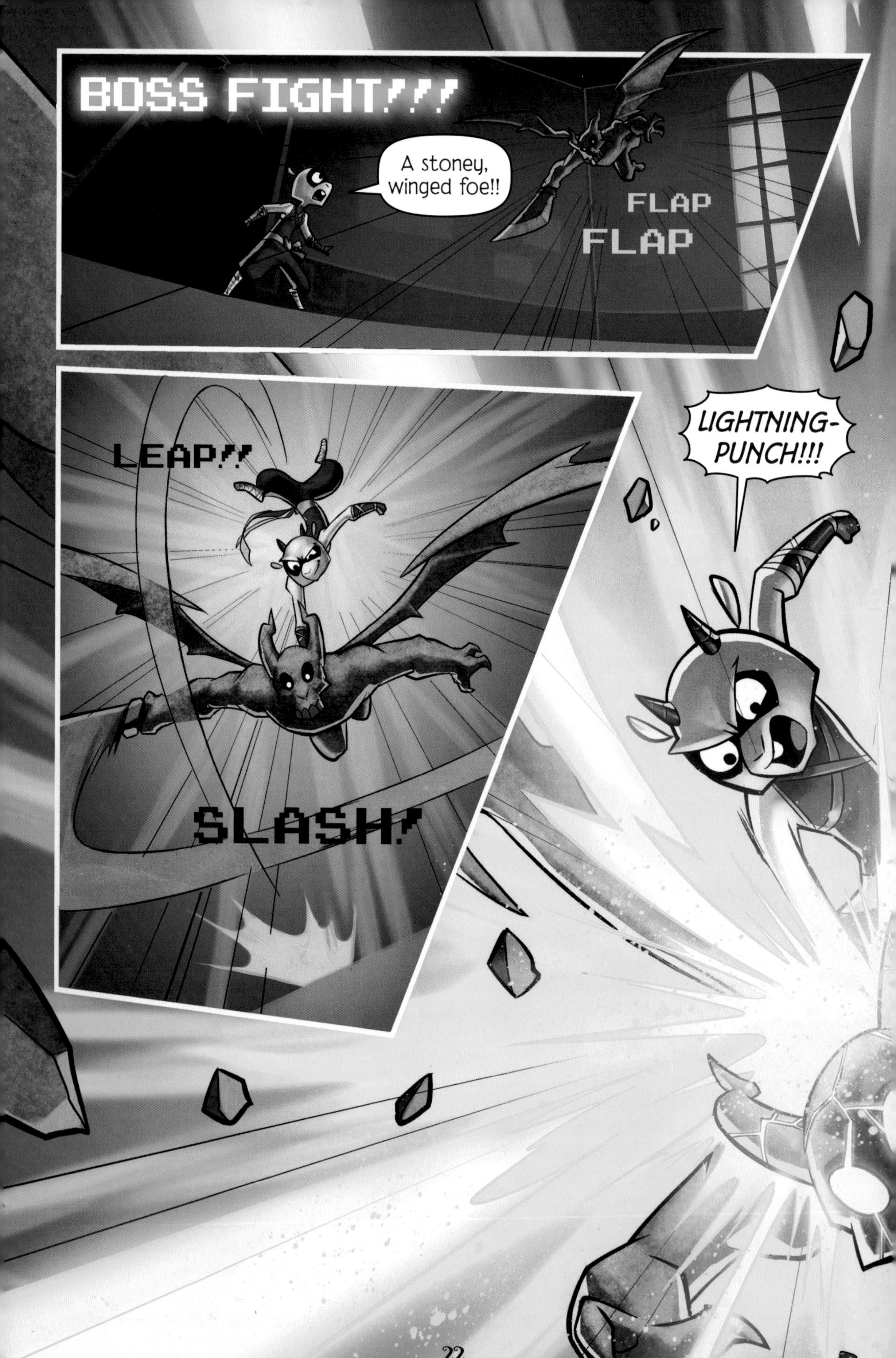
BOSS FIGHT!!!
A stoney, winged foe!!
FLAP
FLAP
LEAP!!
SLASH!
LIGHTNING-PUNCH!!!

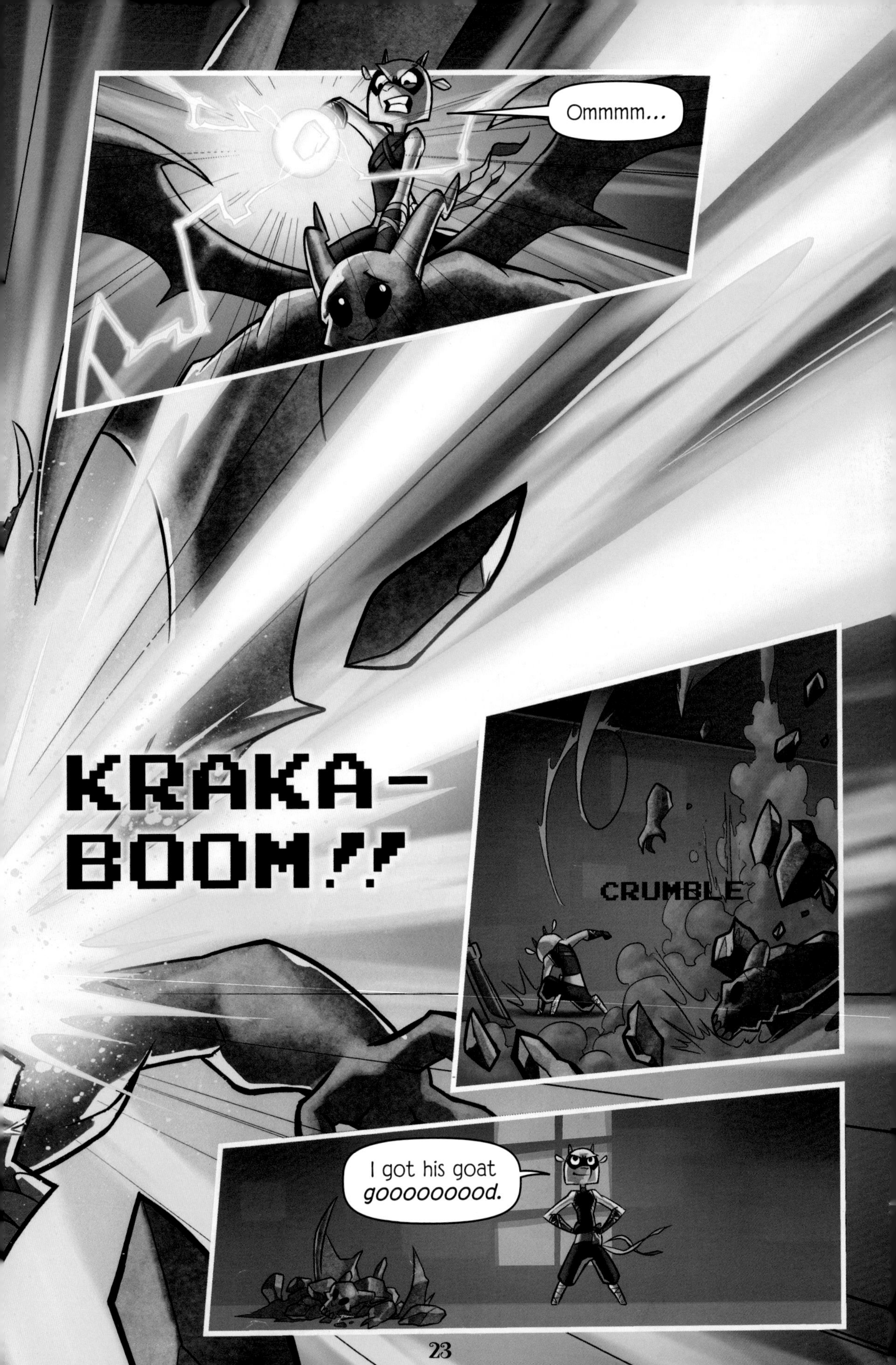
Ommmm...
KRAKA-
BOOM!!
CRUMBLE
I got his goat
gooooooood.

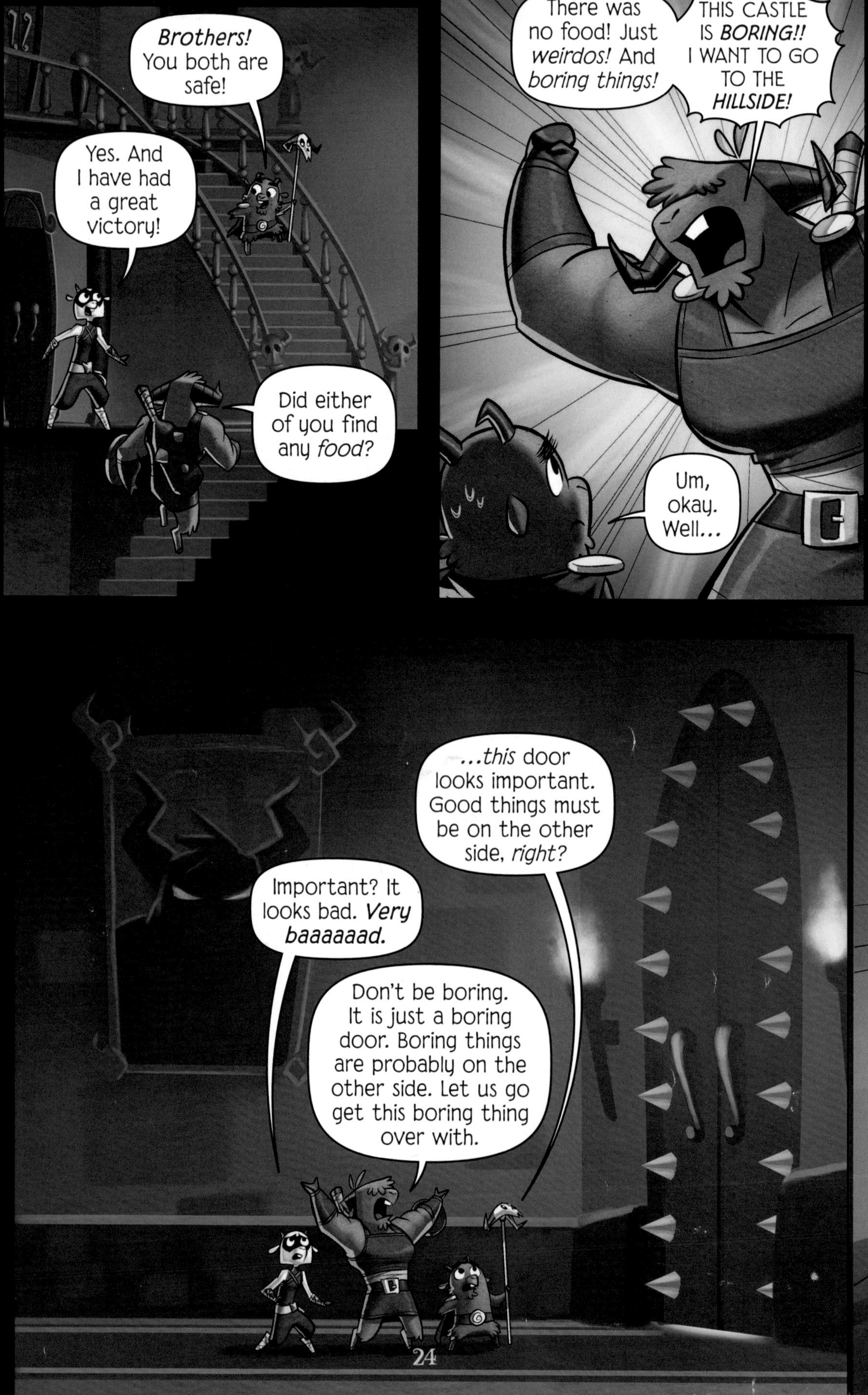
Brothers! You both are safe!
Yes. And I have had a great victory!
Did either of you find any *food?*
There was no food! Just *weirdos!* And *boring things!*
THIS CASTLE IS ***BORING!!*** I WANT TO GO TO THE ***HILLSIDE!***
Um, okay. Well...
...*this* door looks important. Good things must be on the other side, *right?*
Important? It looks bad. ***Very baaaaaad.***
Don't be boring. It is just a boring door. Boring things are probably on the other side. Let us go get this boring thing over with.

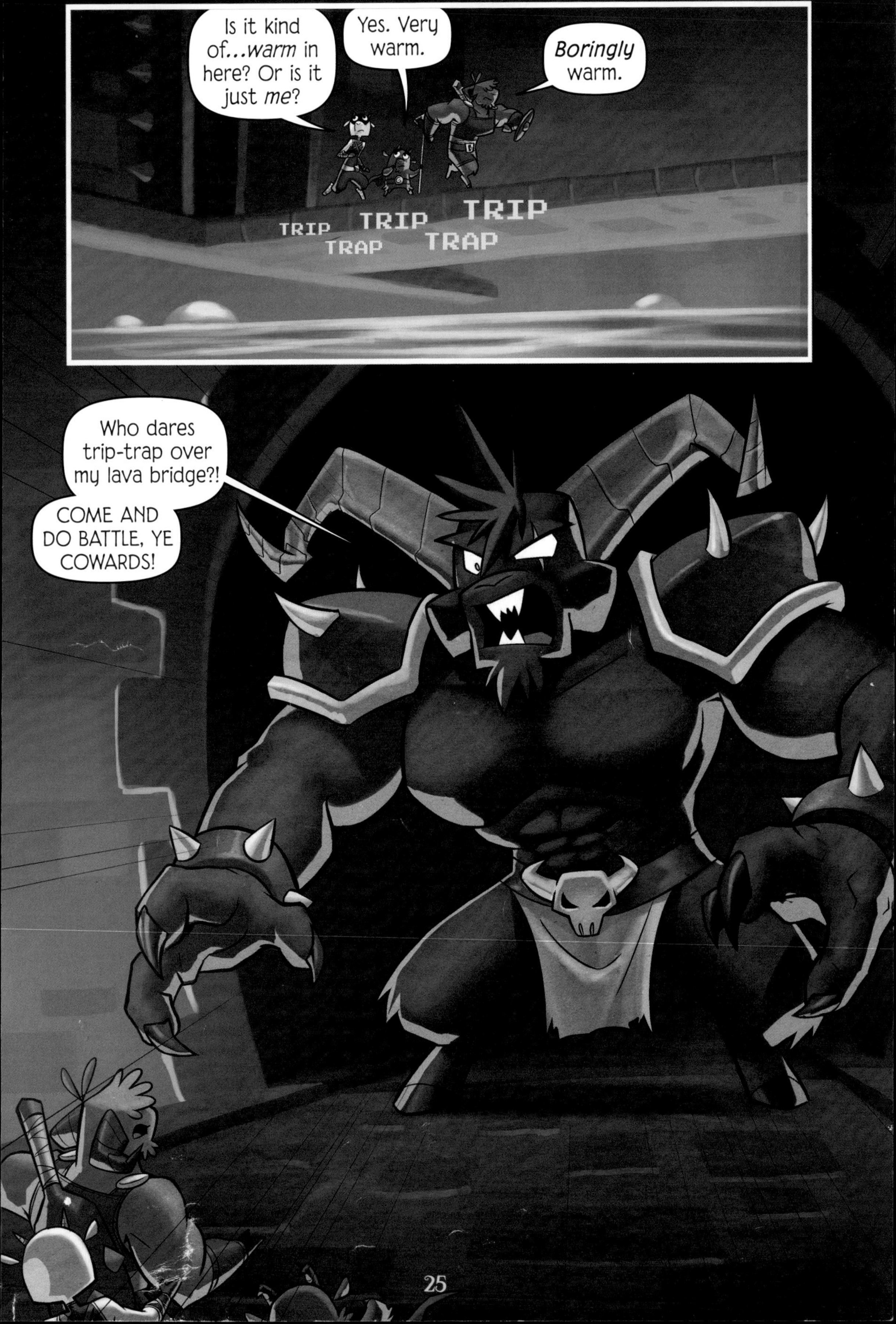
Is it kind of...*warm* in here? Or is it just *me*?
Yes. Very warm.
Boringly warm.
TRIP TRAP TRIP TRAP TRIP
Who dares trip-trap over my lava bridge?!
COME AND DO BATTLE, YE COWARDS!

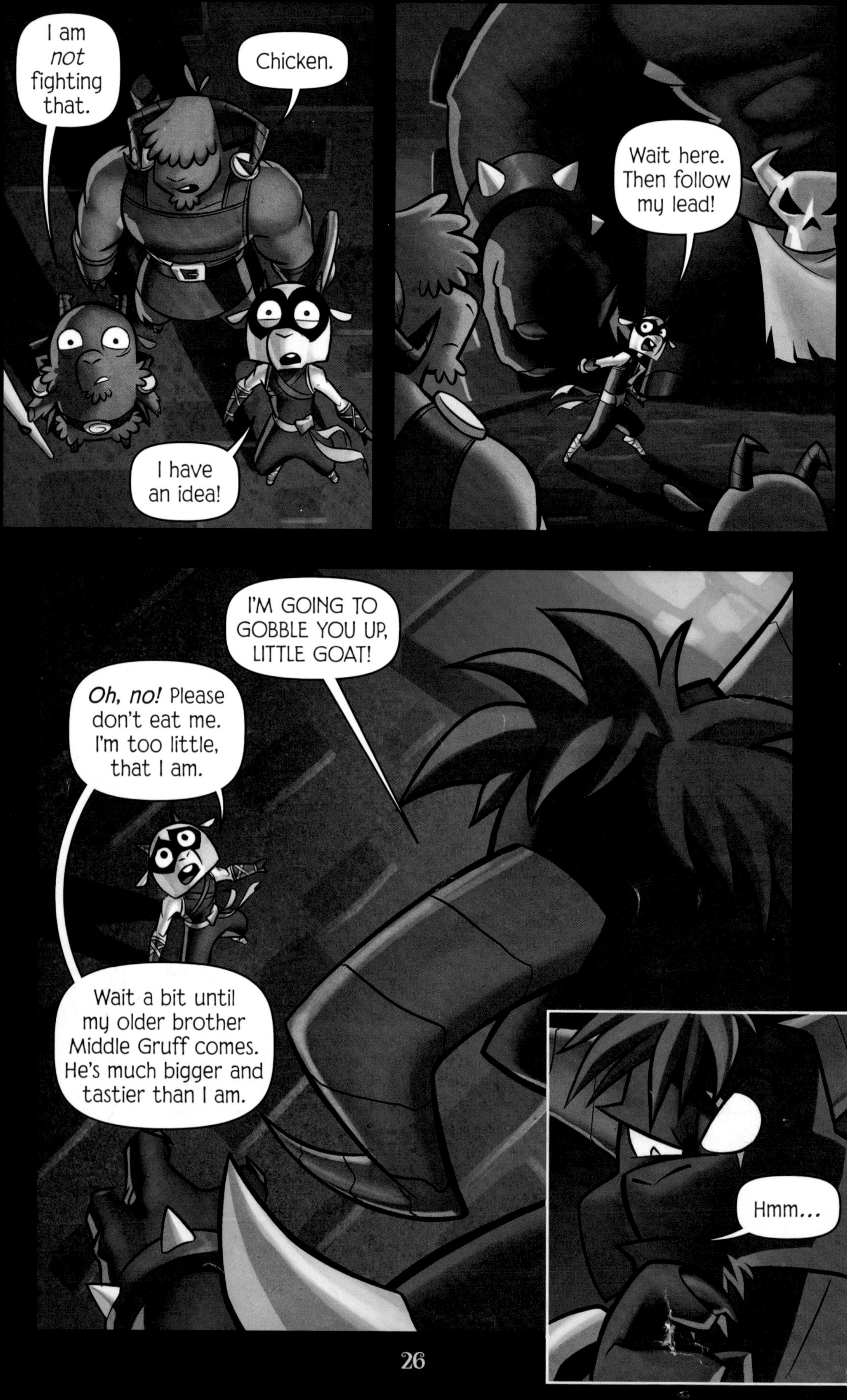

I am *not* fighting that.
Chicken.
I have an idea!
Wait here. Then follow my lead!
I'M GOING TO GOBBLE YOU UP, LITTLE GOAT!
Oh, no! Please don't eat me. I'm too little, that I am.
Wait a bit until my older brother Middle Gruff comes. He's much bigger and tastier than I am.
Hmm...

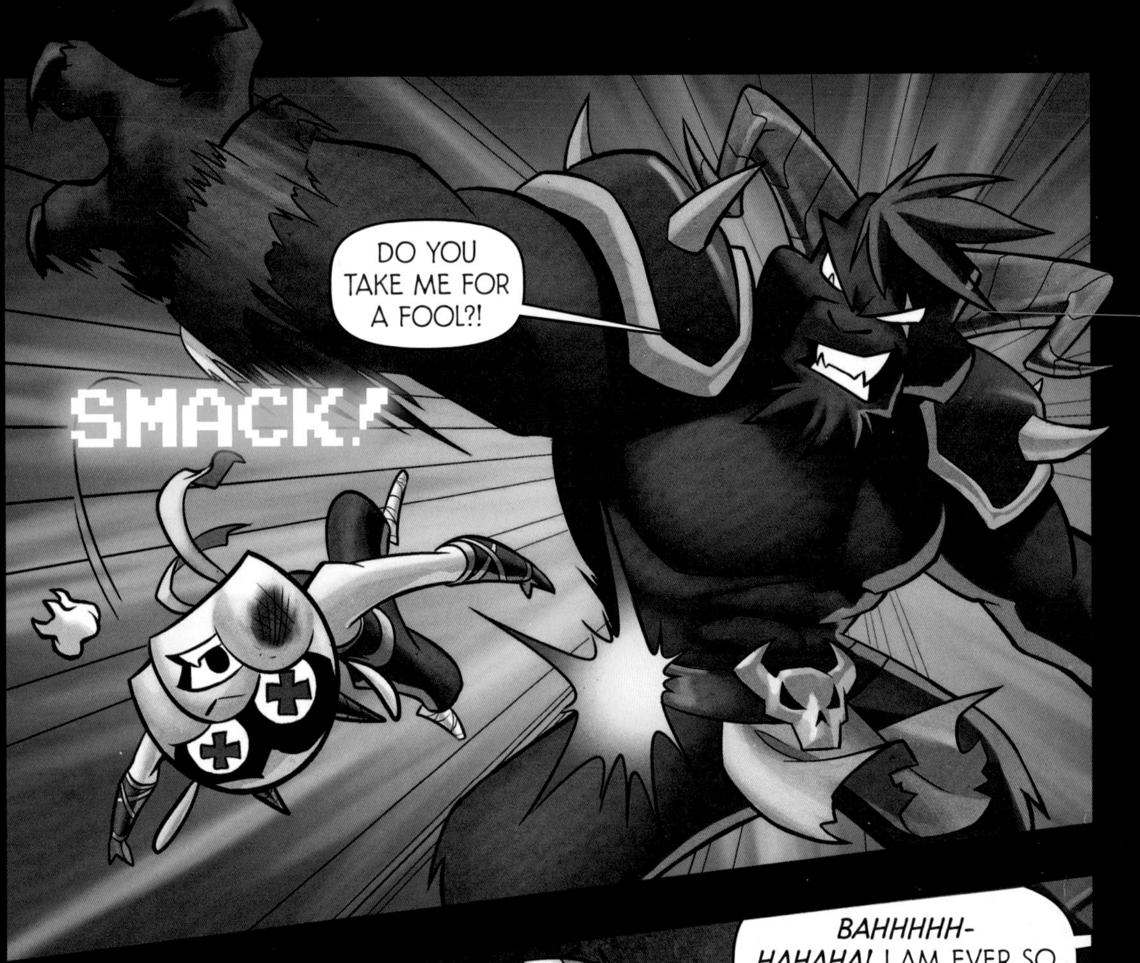
DO YOU TAKE ME FOR A FOOL?!
SMACK!

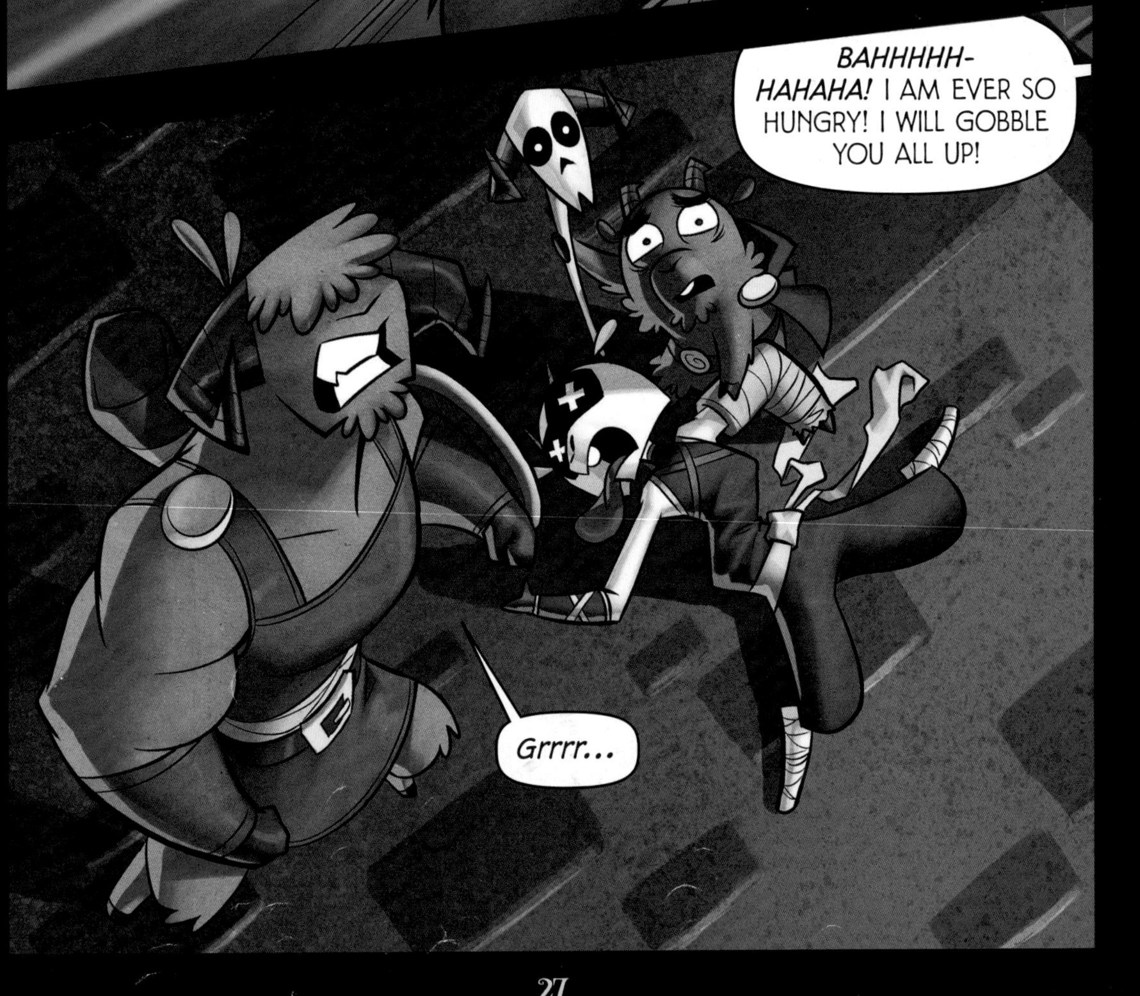
BAHHHHH-HAHAHA! I AM EVER SO HUNGRY! I WILL GOBBLE YOU ALL UP!
Grrrr...

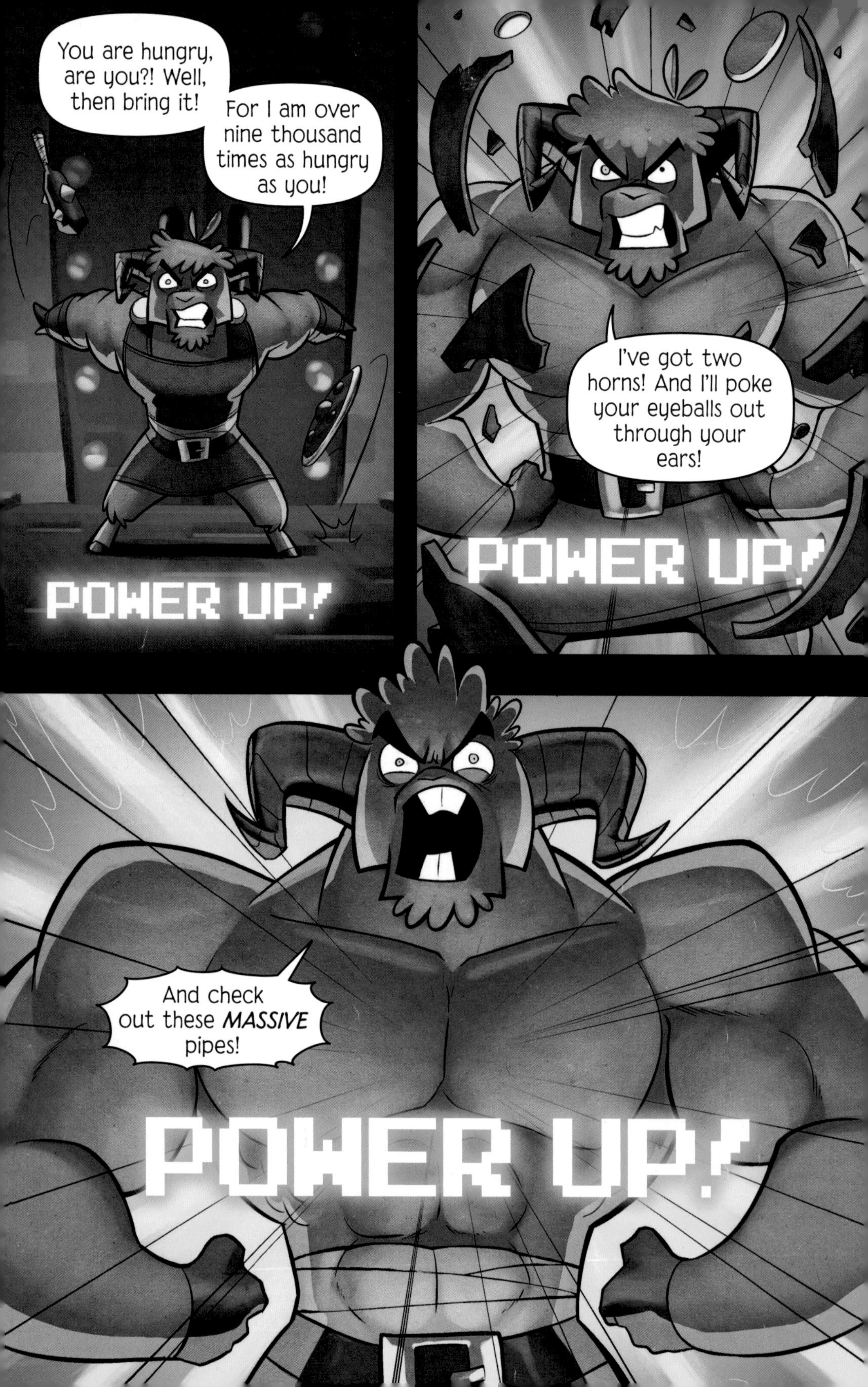
You are hungry, are you?! Well, then bring it!
For I am over nine thousand times as hungry as you!
POWER UP!
I've got two horns! And I'll poke your eyeballs out through your ears!
POWER UP!
And check out these *MASSIVE* pipes!
POWER UP!

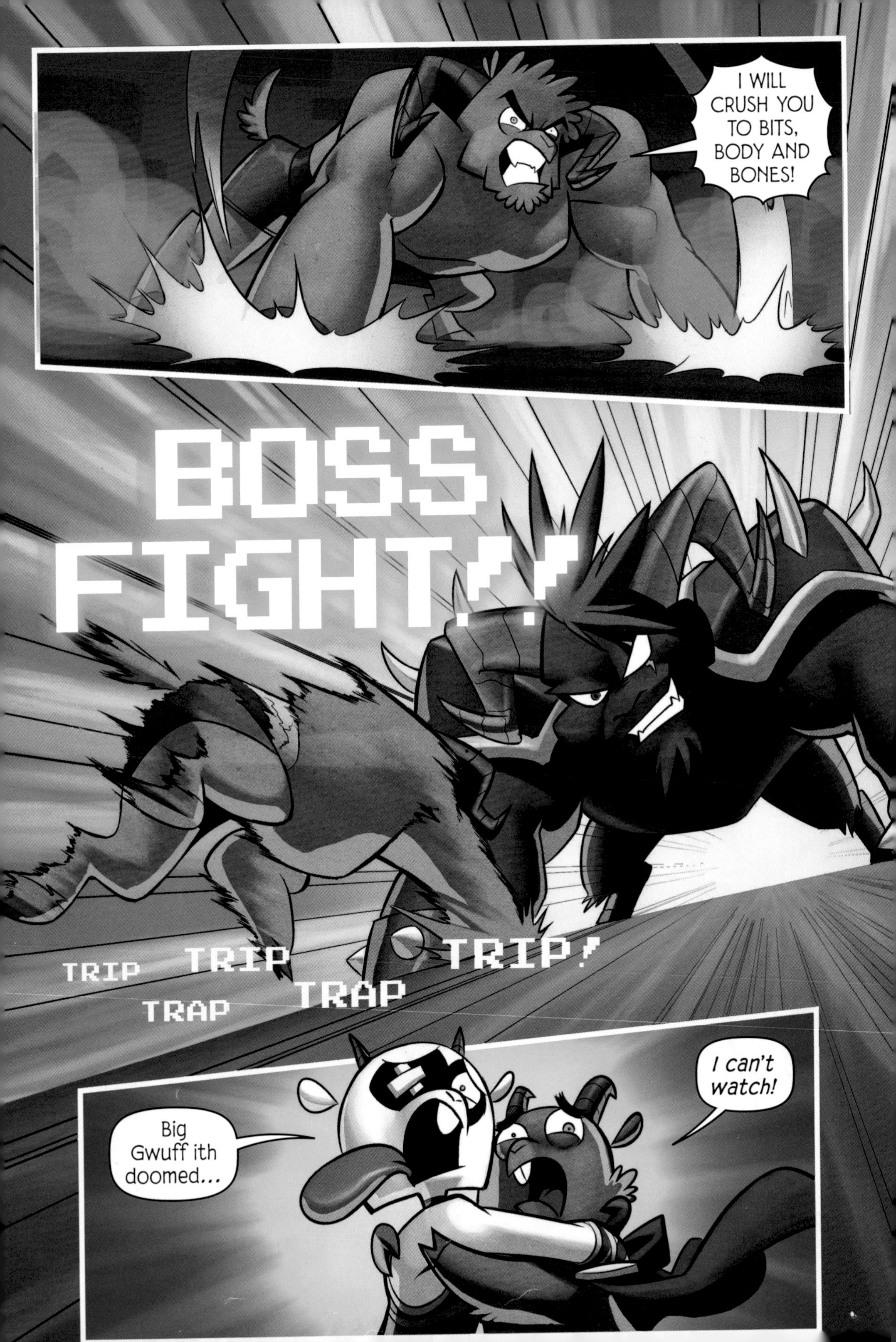
I WILL CRUSH YOU TO BITS, BODY AND BONES!
BOSS FIGHT!!
TRIP
TRIP
TRAP
TRAP
TRIP!
Big Gwuff ith doomed...
I can't watch!

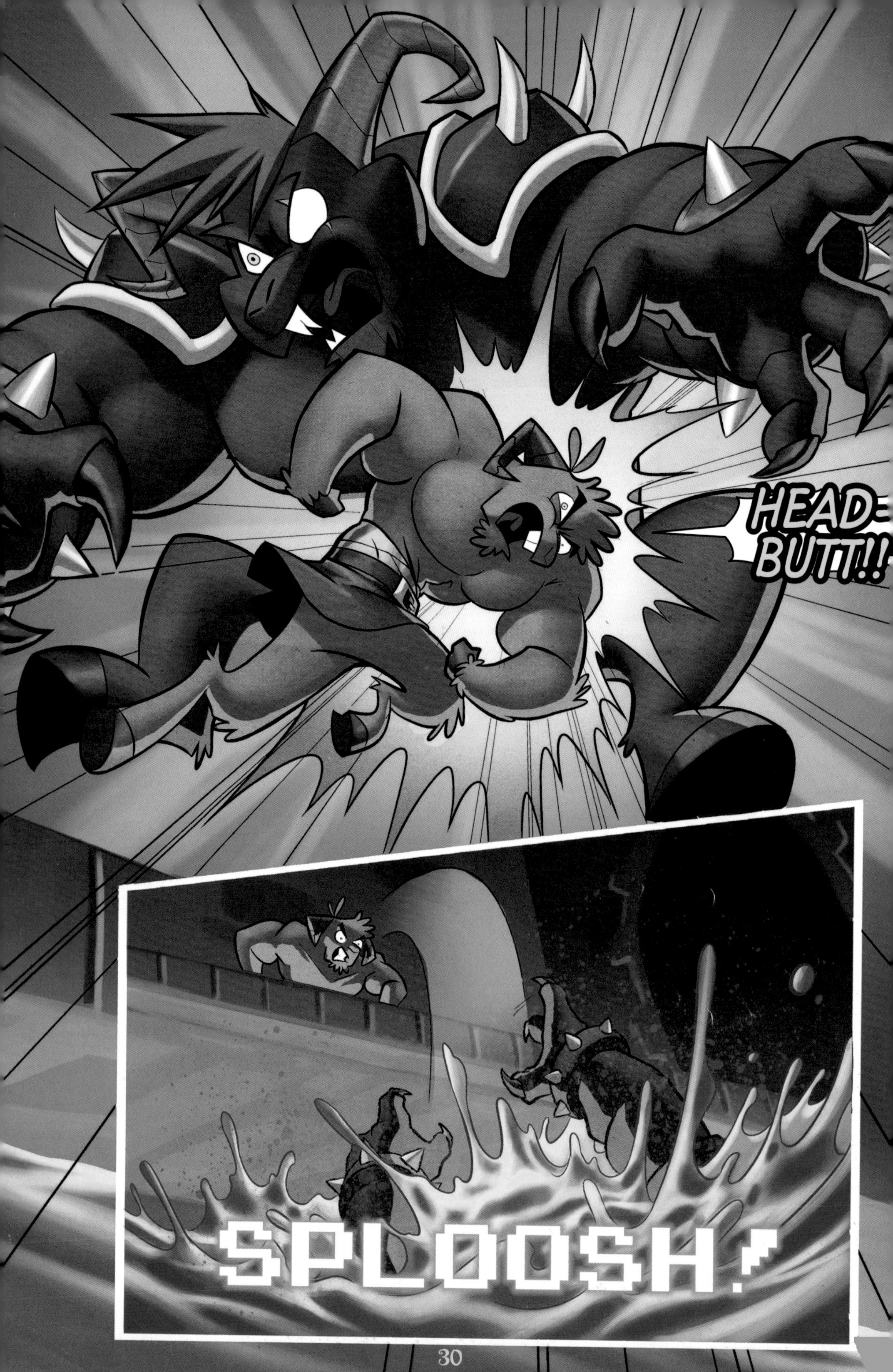
HEAD-
BUTT!!
SPLOOSH!

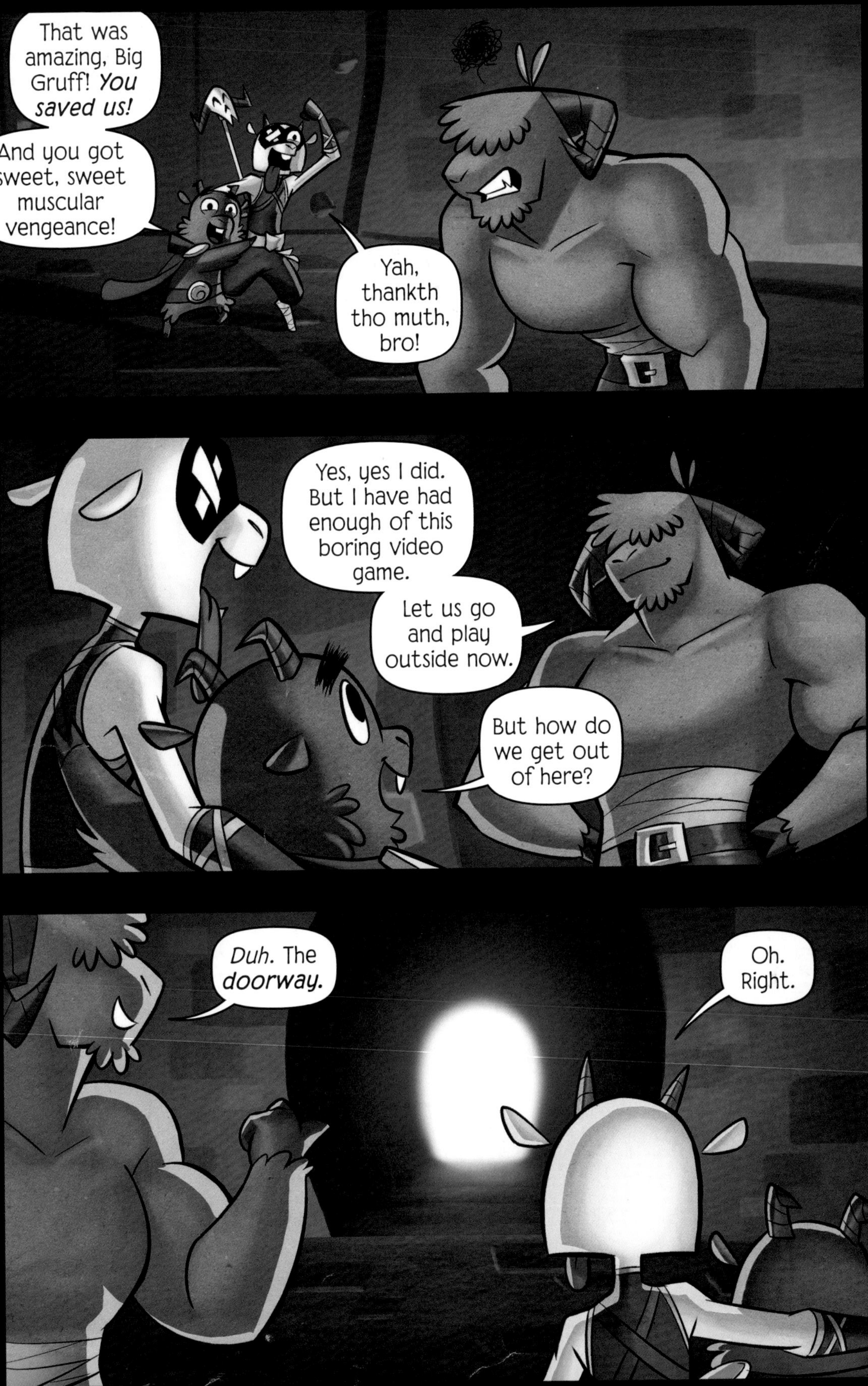
That was amazing, Big Gruff! *You saved us!*
And you got sweet, sweet muscular vengeance!
Yah, thankth tho muth, bro!
Yes, yes I did. But I have had enough of this boring video game.
Let us go and play outside now.
But how do we get out of here?
Duh. The *doorway.*
Oh. Right.

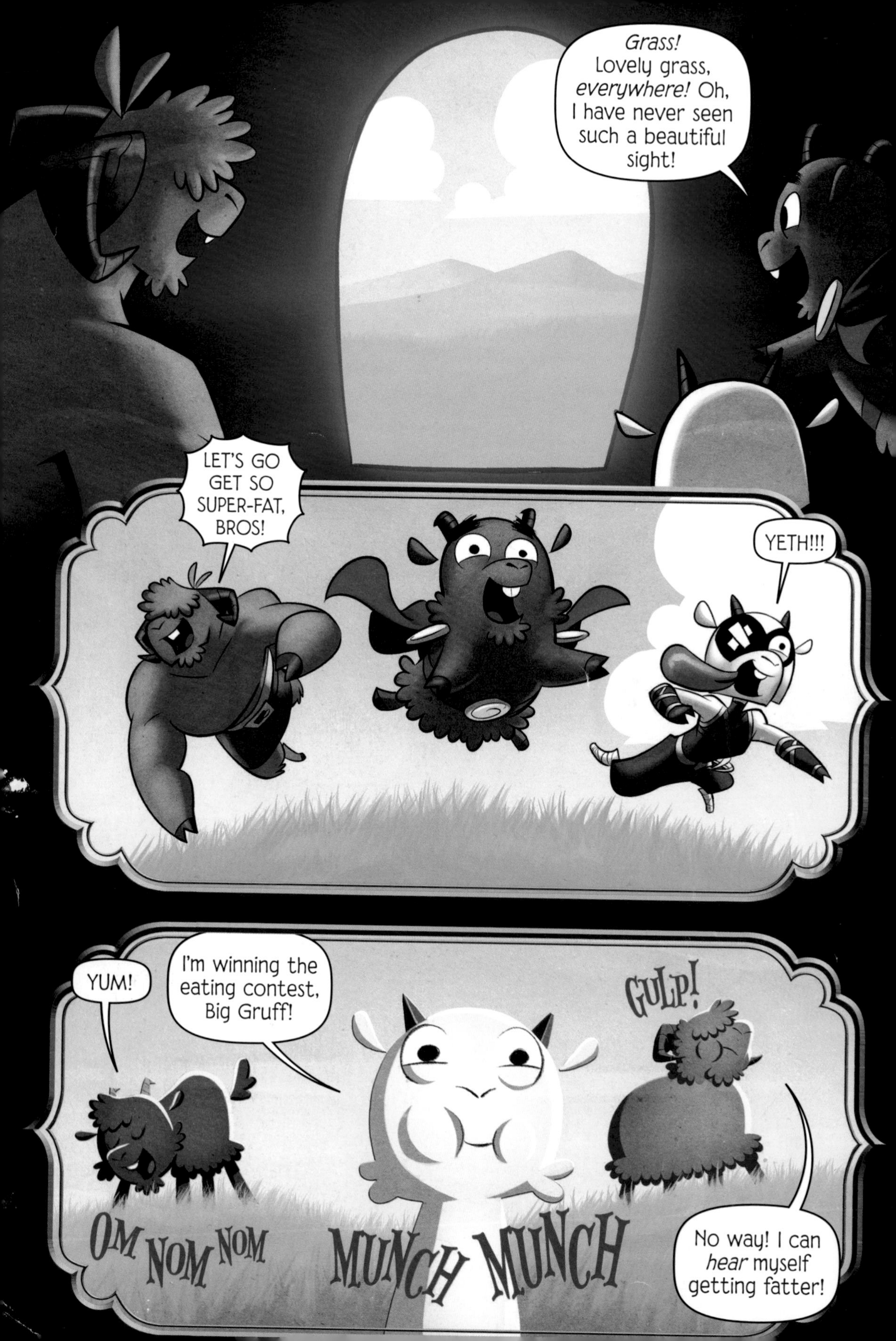

Grass! Lovely grass, *everywhere!* Oh, I have never seen such a beautiful sight!
LET'S GO GET SO SUPER-FAT, BROS!
YETH!!!
YUM!
I'm winning the eating contest, Big Gruff!
GULP!
OM NOM NOM
MUNCH MUNCH
No way! I can *hear* myself getting fatter!

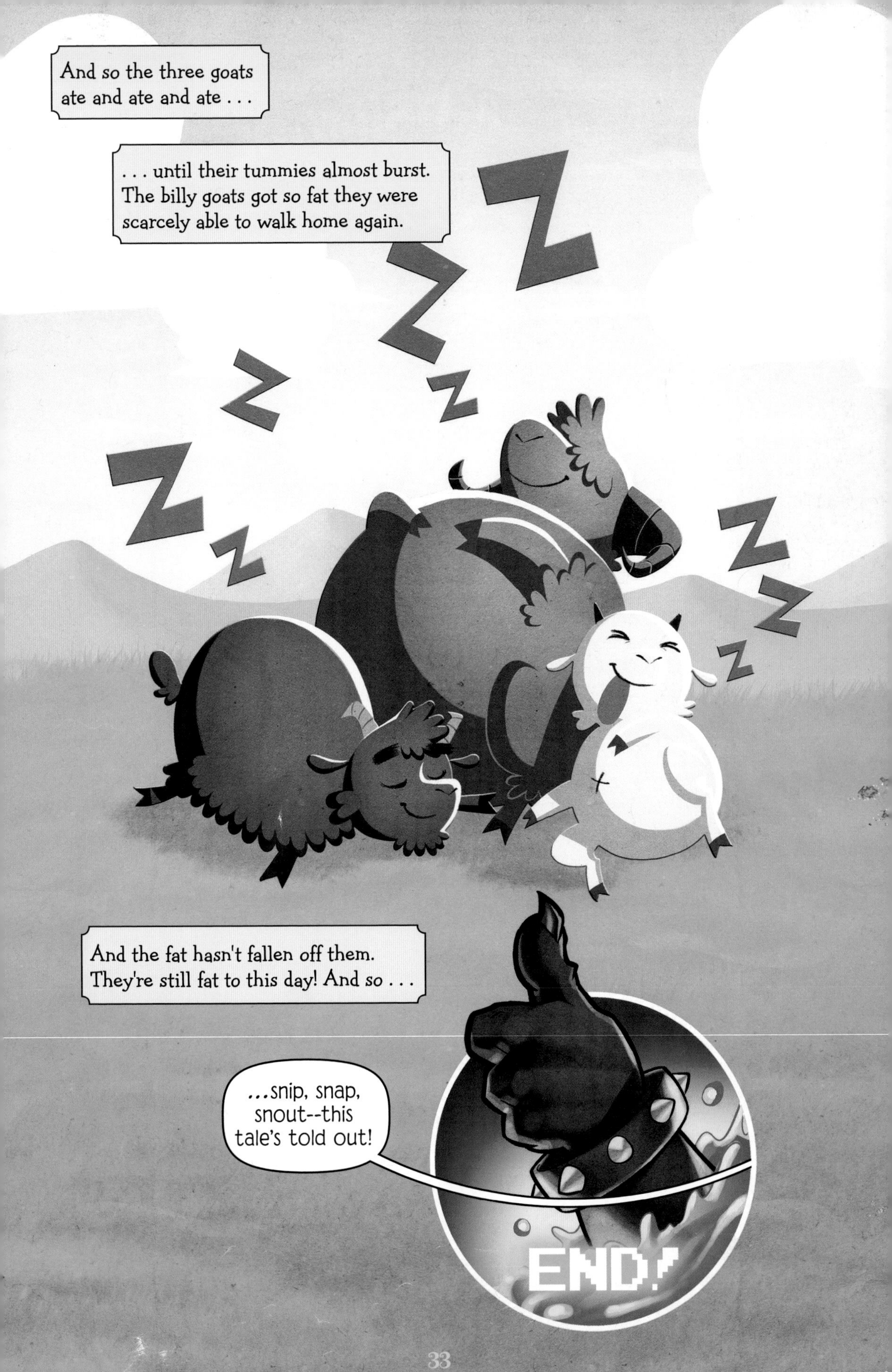
And so the three goats ate and ate and ate . . .
. . . until their tummies almost burst. The billy goats got so fat they were scarcely able to walk home again.
And the fat hasn't fallen off them. They're still fat to this day! And so . . .
...snip, snap, snout--this tale's told out!
END!

ALL ABOUT THE ORIGINAL TALE!

"Three Billy Goats Gruff" is a Norwegian fairy tale first published sometime between 1841 and 1844. While this version has a video game twist to it, the original version has its own far out elements!

The original story introduces three billy goats of different sizes. They are usually referred to as brothers. Hungry for grass, they decide to travel to the hillside across a river in order to eat and get fatter. However, a fearsome troll lives under the bridge that eats anyone who tries to cross.

The smallest billy goat crosses first. When the troll threatens to gobble him up, the little goat tricks him by saying his older, slightly bigger brother would make a better snack and that the troll should wait for him to cross. The greedy troll allows the little goat to pass in hopes of a bigger, better meal.

The middle-sized, slightly larger goat then crosses the bridge. He uses the same trick to get the troll to let him pass, saying that his older, even bigger brother is on his way. It works again.

The third, largest goat is then stopped by the troll, who threatens to gobble him up. But the third goat is so big that he simply kicks the troll off the bridge and into the river! (In some versions of the tale, he bashes the troll to bits with his horns and hooves.)

With the bridge clear, all three goats venture to the hillside, eat their fill of grass, and live happily ever after. The troll continues to live under the bridge but he never bothers anyone ever again.

Super Billy Goats Gruff adds its own weird twists to this timeless tale, including enemies the goats fight before the big battle on the bridge with the Final Boss...

A FAR OUT GUIDE TO HILLSIDE CASTLE!

GRIN-SNEER 💀

BOSS

A shadowy sorcerer, Grin-Sneer summons the skele-goats on the top level of Hillside Castle to fight for him. His father, Tanngrisnir, was one of the Norse god Thor's pet goats. He pulled Thor's chariot and was known for his scary, toothy sneer.

MIMIC $

MINION

It has long been said that greed will lead to the downfall of even the greatest adventurers--and the Mimic is living proof. This hungry chest may apear to hold valuable treasure, but its only contents are the bones of careless adventurers.

GOATGOYLE 💀

BOSS

While most gargoyles serve as rain spouts for buildings, the Goatgoyle only pretends to be a statue. This granite guardian perches atop the roof of the exterior of the castle and serves as the first line of defense against intruders.

FACE-HUGGER ♥

MINION

Some foes are actually friends who just don't understand how to respect personal space. He may mean well, but the Face-Hugger is so needy that he makes it a little hard to breathe-- literally.

VISUAL QUESTIONS

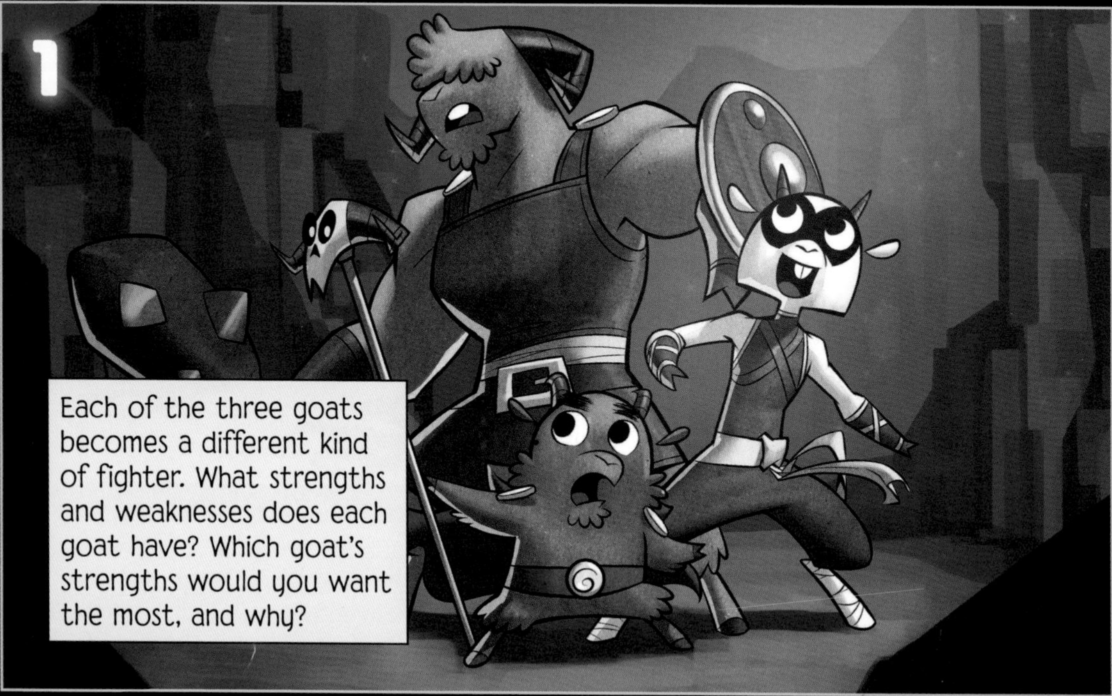

1

Each of the three goats becomes a different kind of fighter. What strengths and weaknesses does each goat have? Which goat's strengths would you want the most, and why?

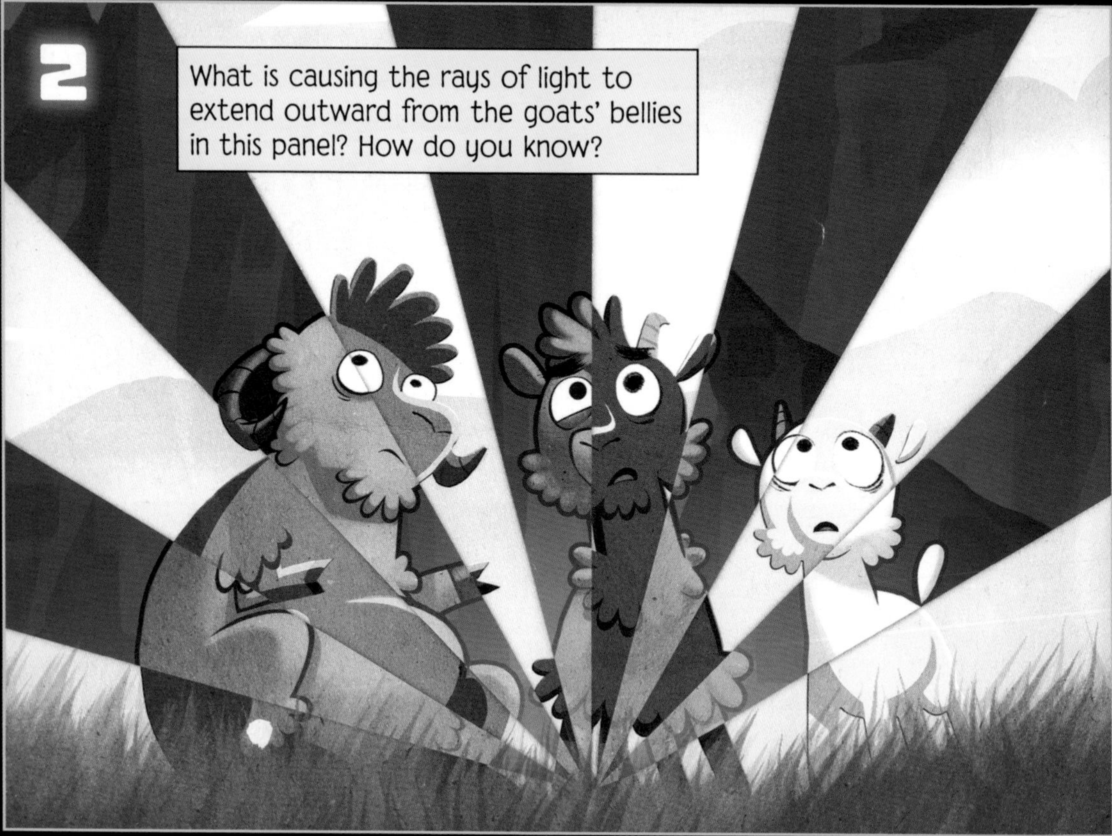

2

What is causing the rays of light to extend outward from the goats' bellies in this panel? How do you know?

3

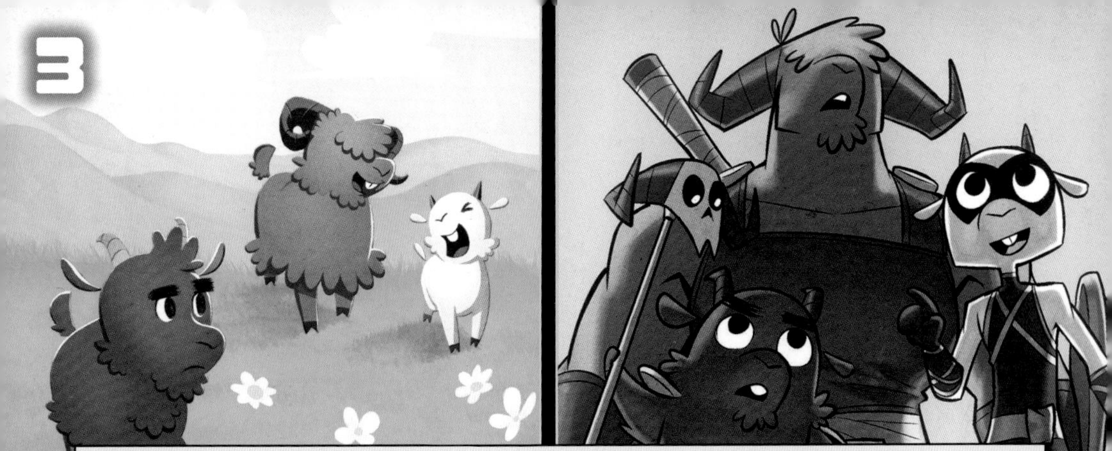

The beginning and end of this comic book have a different illustration style from the middle of the book. Why do you think the comic book's creators chose to do this? When and why does the art style change?

4

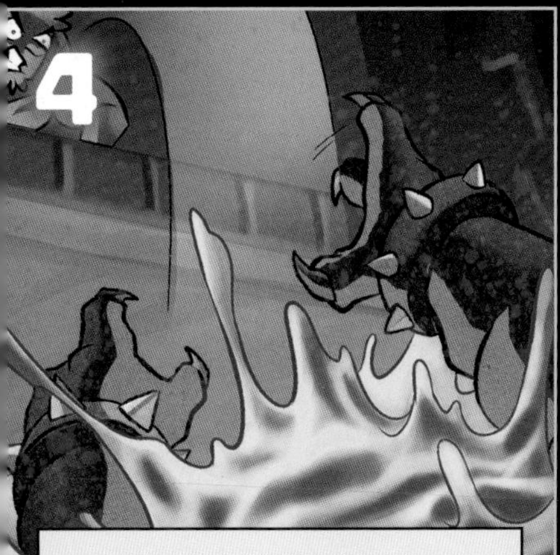

Do you think the Final Boss is still alive? Why or why not? What do you think will happen next in this story?

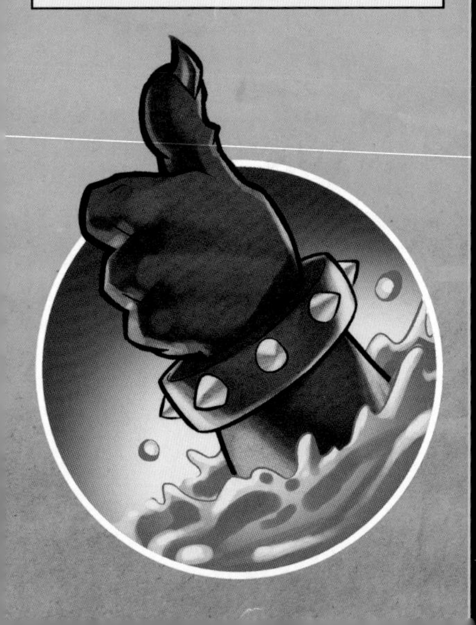

5

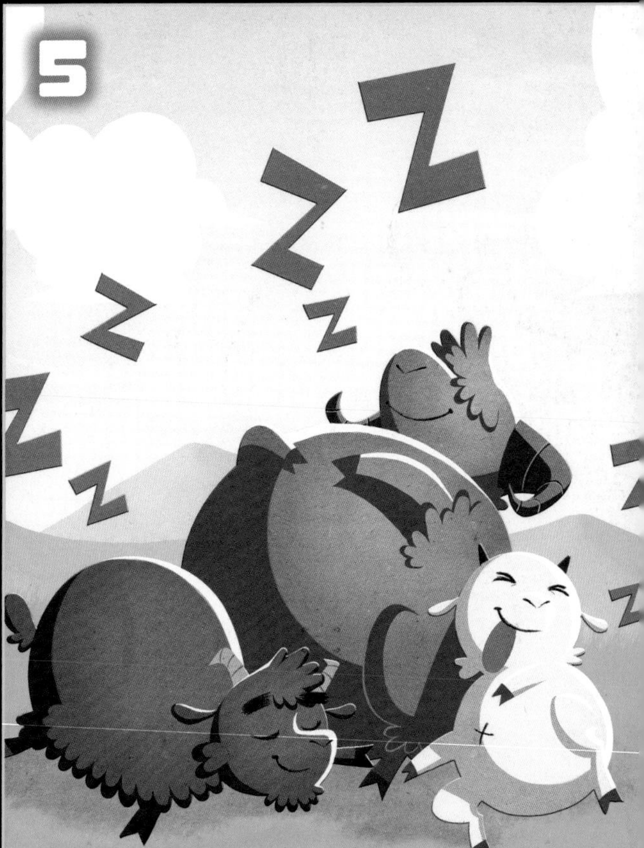

Big Gruff is determined. Little Gruff is quick and curious. Middle Gruff is smart. Which goat is most like you? Write a paragraph about your own personality.

AUTHOR

Sean Tulien is a children's book editor and writer living and working in Minnesota. In his spare time, he likes to read, play video games, eat sushi, exercise outdoors, spend time with his lovely wife, listen to loud music, and play with his pet hamster, Buddy.

ILLUSTRATOR

Fernando Cano is an illustrator born in Mexico City, Mexico. He currently resides in Monterrey, Mexico, where he makes a living as an illustrator and colorist. He has done work for Marvel, DC Comics, and role-playing games like Pathfinder from Paizo Publishing. In his spare time, he enjoys hanging out with friends, singing, rowing, and drawing!

GLOSSARY

challenge (CHALL-uhnj)--if you challenge someone, you test their ability, skill, or strength

cowards (KOW-erdz)--those who are not at all brave or courageous

doomed (DOOMD)--if someone is doomed, they are certain to fail, suffer, or die

gruff (GRUHFF)--rough, course, or very serious in action or speech

massive (MASS-iv)--very large and heavy

ninja (NIN-juh)--a practitioner of the Japanese martial art called ninjutsu. These warriors trained to be sneaky and strike quickly, usually at night.

polymorph (PAHL-ee-mohrf)--a magic spell that changes someone into a harmless creature, or an organism with multiple forms

scarcely (SKAYRSS-lee)--barely, hardly, or not quite

super (SOO-per)--extremely good or awesome

vengeance (VEN-juhnss)--the act of doing something to hurt someone because that person did something that hurt you or someone else you care about

victorious (vik-TOHR-ee-uhss)--having won a victory or having ended in a victory

warrior (WOHR-ee-er)--a person who fights in battles and is known for having courage and skill. Warriors often wear armor and use weapons and sometimes shields.

wizard (WIZ-erd)--a person who is skilled in magic or has magical powers. Wizards can cast spells.

AWESOMELY EVER AFTER.

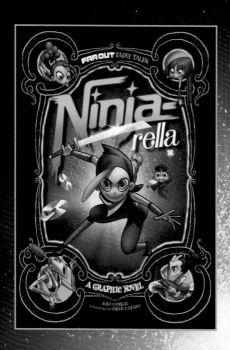

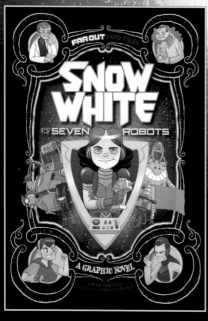

FAR OUT FAIRY TALES

ONLY FROM STONE ARCH BOOKS!